Face-to-Face with What Could Have Been

The vehicle slowly resolved itself into a Jeep Cherokee, and a fairly new, nice-looking one at that. The lack of a front license plate was odd, since Illinois and Missouri required them.

From what Quinn could see of the driver, Cousin Jenny was quite tall.

And had unusually broad shoulders for a woman.

By the time the Cherokee's turn signal flashed for some unknown and oddly hilarious reason out here in the absolute middle of nowhere, Quinn's heart sank and sped up at the same time.

She kept looking at the passenger seat, trying to conjure the woman she'd never seen before. Perhaps accompanied by her husband or son.

But the seat remained empty.

And when the Jeep parked behind her car, Quinn finally stopped pretending.

That was *Doug*.

Even through the dusty windshield, there was no mistaking that smile.

*For the early loves
who help us learn along the way*

THE BOX OF POSSIBILITIES

A SWEET FANTASY ROMANCE

KARI KILGORE

SPIRAL PUBLISHING, LTD.

Chapter 1

THE ONCE-BEAUTIFUL OLD southern Illinois farmhouse had definitely seen better days.

Quinn Hedges leaned back against her generic navy blue work sedan with a dorky realtor logo on the driver side door, trying her level best not to think the same thing about herself in the thirty-three years since she'd last stood in this spot.

A broad expanse of weedy, overgrown grass rustled in the cool October breeze, brushing up against white siding gone more gray with time and dust. Most of the fake black shutters that had been nearly a legal requirement back in the Eighties were still in place.

Like so many things from that gaudy, optimistic era, the remaining shutters hung a little bit broken and crooked in the cool reality of the late Twenty-teens.

Thank goodness the rambling two-story house itself seemed solid enough from the outside. None of the support posts on the wide double porch that surrounded the whole thing were twisted or tilted, and by a small miracle none of the windows she could see were broken.

A sprawling garage/barn combination looked every bit as sturdy, with both overhead doors pulled down and secured with padlocks close to the sloping concrete pad that continued inside. Above the doors, white siding that matched the house extended up to a second story with two broad, unbroken windows with their own black shutters.

She knew without walking around that the barn went back twice as far as the walled-off garage section, and it held more garage doors along one side and a big sliding barn door in the back. The surprisingly comfortable and well-built interior was a fitting home for generations of tinkerers.

Quinn stepped away from the car, absently brushing road dust away from her black long-sleeved t-shirt and the seat of her blue jeans. Perhaps not the best choice for a miles-long drive down farmland gravel, even if it was remarkably well-maintained. But the thought of stepping back into one of the haunts of her teen years left her feeling like that same awkward, insecure kid all over again.

Pulling on a key element of her favorite wardrobe from her thirties and forties before she got on the road this morning helped her remember she was the adult now. Well into her adulthood, in fact, and solidly into middle-age at fifty-one. Just like everyone she remembered from this time and place: some of the most intense and dramatic years of her life.

She turned away from the sad decline of the once-proud family home, facing into the breeze. Someone was burning something, probably brush, though she couldn't see a trace of the smoke against the deep blue sky that dwarfed the house and the land and everything else.

The pale gray line of the gravel road cut through stubbly brown fields, straight as the world's longest arrow all the way to the horizon. Quinn didn't need a map or a GPS or her smartphone to know the whole region was crisscrossed by more of the same lines.

Almost all flat and intersecting at perfect right angles, to the point that any variation from the pattern provided a jarring contrast.

The paved roads were no different most of the time. The novelty of a smooth, easy curve required a veritable forest of warning signs to keep complacent drivers from shooting right through the guardrail into some farmer's back forty.

She clearly remembered her driver's ed teacher explaining how dangerous a curve like that could be, without a trace of irony or humor on his broad, tanned face. Decades of traveling all over the country and a good bit of Europe were her real education in tricky (and exhilarating) driving.

As a stronger gust lifted her short brown hair away from her face, she imagined she smelled the ghosts of bonfires long gone by instead of a distant brush fire. A craving for hotdogs she didn't eat anymore and marshmallow and chocolate s'mores she didn't eat often enough set her stomach to growling. Unfortunately she was a long way away from anything besides corn and soybean fields stripped bare for the winter and an empty house.

A house she'd promised to evaluate and appraise, as a favor for a family who'd always been kind to her, whether she could stand the thought of walking inside or not. In fact, she needed to get herself together and out of her nostalgia haze before the estate executor (and temporary owner) showed up to walk through with her.

Quinn drew in a deep breath to steady herself and promptly sneezed hard enough to stagger back a step. Yep, the return to her native farmlands of Illinois rather than her grownup urban shelter of St. Louis inspired the return of her fierce dust and grass allergies too.

She surprised herself by laughing out loud, then leaned down to check her face in the car's oval side mirror. No damage done other than a little bit of a red rim around her brown eyes. Not all that much damage from all the years passing, either, when she was feeling confident enough to be honest with herself.

A few smile lines around her eyes and mouth. A few scowl lines across her forehead. Enough silver twisting through her hair to look like highlights in the bright afternoon sunlight.

Not bad for a woman a few years past skipping her thirtieth high school reunion.

Shaking her head at her own silliness and dread over the day's activities, Quinn walked through the crunching weeds toward the home of the same family for six proud generations. A family she knew quite well back in those high school days.

About to become the home of strangers she had no desire to know anything about besides signing the papers. She'd agreed to take the job, but flatly and firmly refused any commission for her work. After all the kindness and love she'd experienced here, that would have felt too much like stealing.

It would be all she could manage to keep up her typical light, breezy chitchat with some relative she'd never met, with her own memories rising up so thick and rich in every room.

All things considered, of course, this unknown relative would be a hell of a lot more manageable than walking through with someone she *had* known from the family.

Doug Linton, for example.

Grandson of the sweet people who'd lived in the house back when she spent countless hours here herself.

Doug had also been Quinn's most sincere and serious boyfriend in all her years living nearby. She couldn't properly call him anything other than her first true love, no matter how young they'd been at the time.

And the one whose lovely green eyes always came to mind when melancholy thoughts of what could have been drifted her way.

Chapter 2

SOMETIMES THE BEAUTY of the vast Illinois countryside was impossible to ignore.

The intense, rich blue of the endless sky overhead was stunning all by itself. Only a handful of white, fluffy clouds interrupted the expanse, as if they'd been put there by the special effects department to make that amazing cobalt blue look more realistic.

A driver with a good eye could often pick out red-winged blackbirds perched on the thousands of fenceposts. Glossy black, with a vivid red shoulder patch underlined in yellow, posing like the overseers of the stubbly brown fields dry and empty for winter.

The real overseers were the hawks, though. Much bigger and often on fenceposts of their own. Mottled brown with tan bellies, watching those temporarily desolate fields for mice searching out any lost corn or soybeans.

Then the surprise of a stand of hardwood trees—a twisting snakelike row of them rather than anything as organized as a stand—following along a creek or river too deep or too needed for irrigation to be absorbed by a farmer's ambitions. This time of year, the trees provided a glorious streak of October red and yellow and orange against the distant horizon.

The trail of dust that rose up behind him as the miles of highway gave way to gravel only emphasized the orderly landscape.

Doug Linton laughed under his breath at the way his nervous energy worked itself out in a veritable travelogue of his old stomping grounds. Over twenty years in the comparably wild and unpredictable state of Georgia had tuned his eyes for the near-tropical coast, rolling hills and towering mountains, thick forests, and the bustling city of Atlanta.

Everything he could see here had been transformed to new and exotic.

When he'd fled Illinois not long after high school, he'd been sick to death of the farmlands all around him. Unable to imagine how anyone could possibly find this view tolerable, much less beautiful.

But today, even faced with the sad but necessary chore of getting his beloved grandparents' house ready to sell, all he could see was lovely, fertile land rich with potential.

Maybe the whole day would have potential, if he didn't act all goofy and awkward and like a hopelessly nerdy teenager.

Not the best look for a guy mere weeks from hitting the big five-oh.

Doug shifted in the Jeep Cherokee's seat, glad he'd decided to bring it on the drive despite paying more for gas along the way. His tiny hybrid electric car would have been more sensible, but more than a bit cramped for nearly ten hours. In this case, he happily traded fuel economy for plenty of headroom and legroom for his six-two frame, and a high-end stereo he never would have paid the extra to get.

But he didn't hesitate to enjoy the previous owner's expensive tastes.

Just then, his phone served up not the bright pop of his high school years or the grungy antidote of his twenties. Instead he got music more a part of his parents' generation, and the dreaming orchestral opening to *Knights in White Satin*.

That was the real risk of driving with his phone set to shuffle songs.

The Moody Blues could stab him right through the heart.

Doug reached out his right hand to touch the double-right arrows for skip, then paused.

Maybe this wasn't the time for ignoring those years of his life, and especially that song.

Since he was driving toward an unnerving and not-at-all predictable reunion with the most impor-tant person during all that time, pretending that song didn't exist probably wasn't the best strategy.

Assuming Quinn hadn't decided to cancel at the last minute once the estate's attorney told her about the change of company for this walkthrough.

Doug wasn't yet sure whether to thank his cousin Jenny for calling him a couple of days ago—begging him to fill in because her daughter had just given birth to their first grandchild—or yell at her. Jenny's reasoning that Grandma and Grampa would have chosen *him* for the whole thing instead if he hadn't moved so far away had been just sweet (and true) enough to make up for the blatant manipulation of his feelings.

And of course he'd truly wanted to help and let her have those first few sweet days of grandmother time. He would have done the same if he knew for certain the realtor would be a complete stranger.

He just wouldn't have been nearly so…anxious and carefully excited about it.

He detoured from his phone to pick up the stainless-steel cup that held the fragrant dregs of his late morning coffee fix and finished it off, making a face at how the cold brew tasted foul and sweet at the same time.

He'd now officially managed to get through the bulk of the drive without spilling a thing on his jeans or green flannel shirt despite his lingering little boy fears.

Paranoia made him lean up enough to see the top of his head in the rearview mirror.

Perhaps a little fuzzy with the dry air contrasting with Atlanta's humidity, but not the staticky mess he'd been afraid of.

He'd abandoned the goofy mullet hairstyle of his youth as the Eighties gave way to the Nineties. Now photos of himself from back then made him cringe, with their undeniable proof of his short trim everywhere but the back of his neck. There the corkscrews were free to twist and twirl all the way to his shoulders.

After such indignities, decades later he was grateful his hair hadn't abandoned him. Sure, his curly red locks had lost quite a bit of that intense color. But he only had a scattering of gray creeping in around the edges.

The gray was mostly confined to his beard, which wasn't his favorite sign of aging. Shaving left him looking too much like that mulleted teenager to contemplate. Keeping it trimmed down to a goatee took care of most of that and showed off the ginger shades he had left.

For now.

He'd eventually have to deal with the inevitable fade and move on.

He'd spent the night in Clarksville, Tennessee, north of the traffic and rush of Nashville, so he'd only been wearing his contacts for about five hours. He should easily be able to get through the walk-through of the house before switching them out for the trendy little wire-framed glasses he'd finally admitted he needed when he turned forty.

Another fidgety glance in the mirror confirmed his eyes hadn't taken on the reddish, irritated look of dryness just yet.

So far so good with only a few minutes to go.

The song shifted to the spoken word section—fantastic to listen to and in the impossible-to-dance-to category for sure.

That hadn't stopped him and Quinn from doing their best to dance as long as they could, to this or any other song. On the creaky wooden floor of the high school gym, at an outdoor concert on the grassy lawn. In his bedroom when his parents were out of town.

Figuring out how they fit together in their minds, hearts, and bodies had been so easy. So effortless. Leaving both of them convinced that meant it would last forever. How could it not?

And it did, until it didn't.

Until they each made their own decisions and went in their own directions.

Not because they didn't still love each other. That part never wavered.

Life just…took both of them away from each other. He hadn't understood why they couldn't make it work then any more then he could now.

Doug shook his head, relieved after all when Duran Duran brought the joyful exuberance of *Rio* out to lighten his mood.

Just one more turn and a couple miles more, and he'd have at least one part of his occasional daydreams play out in real life.

He'd see Quinn Hedges again for the first time in over thirty years.

And see if his hopes of at least rekindling their friendship that had followed him across so much time would survive the transition to reality.

Chapter 3

QUINN FINISHED her walk around the house, pleased and amused at having survived the rigors and surprises of a long-untended Illinois landscape.

No snakes, thank goodness, and no wasps or hornets that would have been sluggish and angry in the cool air. That was one of the many reasons she was in the habit of wearing heavy hiking boots for jobs like this.

But she'd startled a rabbit nearly under her feet despite the crackling weeds, stepped through a clay flowerpot long-since grown over, and kicked up more than enough fluffy white seed pods and yellow bursts of pollen to keep her sinuses complaining for days to come.

The far side of the house was in fairly good shape, and she'd been able to get close enough to peek into a few windows without going up on the porch. She hated leaving footprints near entryways before the family's representative arrived.

Inside the house, it looked eerily like the Lintons

had been there for breakfast, or dinner the night before at the latest. Then vanished with no trace.

Furniture not much different than she remembered, with touches like a bookmarked novel never to be finished and a colorful half-knitted...something...to drive the sadness that much deeper.

She knew from the notes about this job that Mrs. Linton had lived here on her own for years after her husband passed, with family members taking turns staying with her. After a nasty fall a couple of years ago, she'd finally moved into assisted living in a nearby town. A reluctant concession to the closest hospital being more than an hour away.

Quinn got the impression no one had the heart to deal with the house until she finally passed a few months back.

She walked toward her car, again brushing her clothes to remove assorted natural debris, then stopped, peering down the expanse of empty farmland.

A plume of gray dust was settling off to the right of the main road, where she'd turned herself when she arrived. Unknown Cousin Jenny most likely, and promising to be right on time.

Sure enough, a burgundy vehicle appeared with the same dusty flourish behind it.

Quinn peeked into the car's mirror one more time, making sure she didn't look like she'd just sneezed five or six good ones. Then she opened the back door to grab a travel pack of tissues and her little spiral notebook, an old-school backup to her smartphone that she never had managed to give up.

The vehicle slowly resolved itself into a Jeep Cherokee, and a fairly new, nice-looking one at that.

The lack of a front license plate was odd, since Illinois and Missouri required them.

From what she could see of the driver, Cousin Jenny was quite tall.

And had unusually broad shoulders for a woman.

By the time the Cherokee's turn signal flashed for some unknown and oddly hilarious reason out here in the absolute middle of nowhere, Quinn's heart sank and sped up at the same time.

She kept looking at the passenger seat, trying to conjure the woman she'd never seen before. Perhaps accompanied by her husband or son.

But the seat remained empty.

And when the Jeep parked behind her car, Quinn finally stopped pretending.

That was *Doug*.

Even through the dusty windshield, there was no mistaking that smile.

Quinn smiled in return despite her shock, and her sincere awareness that she was entirely unprepared to deal with this today only deepened and took over the rest of her body.

She forced herself to start walking on legs that never seemed to touch the ground, trying to thread the needle between placing her feet deliberately so she wouldn't stumble and taking such care with each step that she overshot and walked like a drunk.

Her arms and chest responding with an almost painful burst of hot tingling that surely reflected in her face only intensified the effect.

The door opened, and she realized all her daydreams of how her first love would have grown into a man had fallen far short of the reality.

He had to be a foot taller, and those strong, broad

shoulders hadn't been an illusion. His green flannel shirt highlighted how much lovely red lingered in his beard and hair.

The way the shirt was comfortably tucked into his jeans made it clear he'd escaped the trap of softening into middle age, or he'd never fallen into it in the first place.

And he still had the same sweet, joyful smile, though he looked more than a little shy and hesitant right now.

Oh.

Probably because Quinn had slowed to a stop before she got to the front end of the Jeep. Better not to try to move again and lurch forward like a demented zombie.

"I wish I could think of something clever to say," she said, amazed that her voice only trembled a little. "But I'm going with I didn't expect to see you here."

Doug's smile vanished and he drew back, adding an adorable flush to his cheeks along with his dismayed expression.

"I thought…the attorney was supposed to warn you. Or, *tell* you, I mean, let you know plans had changed. Jenny couldn't make it, well, obviously she couldn't since she's not here. She's my first first cousin to become a grandparent if you can believe that, and she asked me to help. I wanted a road trip, so yeah. And I'm babbling now."

He put his hands on his hips and stared at the gravels underfoot.

"I'm so sorry to just appear like this, Quinn. That wasn't how I hoped this would go."

Apparently Quinn's nervous laughter problem from her teenage years resurfaced here too, because that's exactly what she did. At least he smiled a little instead of looking like he'd accidentally kicked over a kid's prized art project or something equally horrible.

She shook her head and got herself into motion with only a trace of the dreaded zombie shuffle.

"It's okay, you don't have to apologize. I never did get the message from the attorney. She probably didn't think a change of personnel would make that much of a difference."

From only a couple of feet away, she could see how kind the years had been to him. Unfairly kind, really. He hardly seemed to have aged at all, aside from the vivid red of his hair fading to more of an auburn. Only a few smile lines around his eyes and mouth seemed to mark so many years going by.

How could he possibly be even better looking?

"It's good to see you, Doug."

Quinn stepped forward at the same time he did, holding out both of her arms for a hug.

Nearly colliding with his outstretched hand before they both drew back.

She managed to grab his hand before they could reverse positions and make this whole thing even more painfully awkward. His grip was warm and strong, and she let go before she was ready.

"Your cousin is a grandmother now?" she said. "Is it possible we're that old?"

Doug laughed, and a tiny bit of the discomfort fell away. That had been the heart of their relationship, even more than the irresistible physical attraction.

They talked and laughed constantly, their minds every bit as much in love as the rest of them.

"Afraid so," he said, leaning against his Jeep with

his arms crossed. "The Grand Master of the Universe, otherwise known as Ian, arrived about a week early. So our generation has officially crossed the line into being grandparents. I'll be fifty in December, which I have to say has not sunk in for me at all yet."

Quinn rolled her eyes, focusing on a glimpse of the unbelievably blue sky to make sure she wasn't staring at Doug hard enough to freak him out.

"You might remember that I turned fifty-*two* last month. I can verify that it's strange, but survivable. You don't look anywhere near it, if that helps."

Before Quinn could dissolve into a puddle over what had just come out of her mouth, or maybe scurry back to her car and try to escape across the open fields, Doug shook his head and waved one hand toward her.

She didn't miss the shy smile she remembered so well.

"Oh, well, thank you for saying so anyway. You look wonderful, Quinn. I really am sorry about surprising you like this."

Quinn took a deep breath, determined to remember who she was now, and all the years that stood between her and this man. Daydreams and what-ifs aside, she was here to do a job, and a favor to a family who'd always been incredibly kind to her.

Not to fall back into an often-repeated dance with an old flame that always ended up the same way.

No screaming fights, no drama to speak of. Just the two of them getting together, moving in rhythm for a little while, and drifting apart even though neither of them seemed to understand why or want the separation.

Again.

"No need to apologize," she said. "Not when it comes to seeing old friends after too many years have passed, right? I hope we can catch up before you head back to…"

He nodded and rubbed his forehead, then ran his fingers through his hair. A habit that hadn't changed since he was a teenager.

"Atlanta. I'll be heading back to Atlanta. I'd love to catch up whenever we're done here."

"Okay. Let's see what kind of shape the house is in and talk about what you and your family want to do about it."

Chapter 4

Doug kept what he hoped was a respectable, believable smile on his face until Quinn turned away. Then he couldn't stop his shoulders from slumping and his face from surely doing worse.

What had he been *thinking*, just showing up out of nowhere like this?

What had he expected, or even hoped for?

All he'd managed so far was springing what was obviously an unwanted and unpleasant surprise on someone who meant a lot to him. Probably making a fool of himself in the process.

He couldn't keep his eyes away from her now any more than he had when they were both inexperienced kids. Learning with and from each other. Supposedly figuring out what they'd each want from their adult relationships going forward.

Think about it as practice for *the real thing*—that was what his parents and friends told him, and he eventually told himself.

Don't let one breakup be the end of the world,

man. No matter how many times they were drawn back together again before he left the whole state and even the Midwest for good.

Look at the whole thing as practice and plan to do better next time.

Too bad he'd spent decades discovering nothing and no one else ever quite lived up to what he'd had with Quinn.

Over the last couple of years he hadn't much bothered to try.

Of course she had to be even more gorgeous now than she'd been back then. Her strong, angular body had taken on a softness that suited her. Same with her amazing wavy hair. The sparkles of silver mixed in with the hundred shades of brown only high-lighted how lovely it was.

Even her voice—always deep and smooth—had improved somehow. Now she spoke with confidence and resonance that only made sense with growing up and into the woman she wanted to be.

And all of that and how it affected Doug mattered not in the slightest. Not if Quinn really was perfectly fine with him going back to Atlanta and disap-pearing from her life before he could become part of it again.

He followed her, noticing her sedan with a realtor decal on the door was from Missouri. Thousand-to-one odds that meant St. Louis, where she'd always talked about wanting to live. Just far enough away from her family and her past, she always said, but a whole different world.

Not far enough away for him, as it turned out. He'd needed over five hundred miles to start to find his footing in the adult world.

"You have the key?" he said, a second before he realized what a silly question it was. Of *course* the realtor had the key.

She was kind enough to smile instead of laughing at him as she held up a little paper rectangle, probably with the address or something like that written on it. Three silvery keys flashed in the sunlight, hanging from a tiny little keyring. Not all that different from what he'd seen on his own house searches down south.

"Got them right here," she said. "The place could use a little cleaning up outside, but it looks like it's in great shape. Your attorney said the power is still on, too."

"Yeah, Jenny stopped by when she could, and I know the neighbors at least drive by. This house always did have good bones."

Doug bit his lip, stopping his mouth but not his mind from continuing the thought.

That's how they'd ended things, that last time. With a long, painful conversation, all about how their love had good bones.

A solid foundation for sure.

Even as they held each other tight, they at least pretended to agree that sometimes all those things just weren't enough.

Quinn stepped lightly up two concrete steps onto the porch, leaving the first set of footprints in dust thick enough to make Doug's heart clench. She fitted one key into the side door's deadbolt and turned, then the second into the doorknob, as if she'd last walked inside a couple of days ago instead of half a lifetime ago.

"It's a fantastic house, Doug. I always loved it

here." He started forward, but she held up one hand. "Take it from me, you won't want to go charging inside just yet. No matter how good it looks on the outside, it's going to be musty. Let it air out a bit first."

One breath proved her point, when a thick wave of closed-off, stale reek he was surprised he couldn't actually see rolled out. A painful change from a house that always smelled like cinnamon and vanilla and all manner of other delicious things in his mind.

He stepped back and looked toward the left, where the wide porch continued on and disappeared around the front of the house and the front door only people who'd never been there before used. The huge porch swing his great-grandfather made had hung in that corner since before he was born.

"I hope the swing is inside," he said, "or maybe out in the barn. I'd hate to think of someone carrying it off."

Quinn stepped away from the door herself, and her friendly, open smile and sparkling eyes set off an all-too-familiar reaction in Doug's belly. A slow-rolling warmth like a sultry late evening breeze in deep-summer Georgia.

"It would take a crew of someones to carry that swing off, as solidly built as it is. Doesn't look like anything has been broken or vandalized, so I'd bet nothing has been stolen. I'm guessing it's only out of sight. We'll just have to find it."

He smiled, trying not to read too much into her words. They'd discovered all kinds of things on that swing.

"Think it's safe to go inside?" he said. "From the stink, I mean."

"I think it will be fine if we open windows as we go. Just have to remember to close them again before we're finished." She tilted her head and stared at him, with a faint scowl that cooled off his middle in a heartbeat. "Listen, I don't know much about what you and your family are planning to do with the house. Do you have a buyer in mind or anything like that?"

Doug brushed the toe of his hiking boot across the smooth, white-painted boards, leaving a dustless streak.

"I wish… I wish I could tell you we plan to keep it. Make sure it's available to everyone for visits, and to bring their kids to see where we all came from. We'd probably wait a lot longer if any of us thought it made sense, but we need to find someone who wants to live here. Otherwise it really will fall apart. And that would be a damn shame, you know?"

His voice and expression must have been more gloomy than he intended. Sadness etched Quinn's face as she walked forward and reached for his hand. He held hers lightly and resisted the intense urge to pull her forward into a hug, like the one he'd been too boneheaded to realize she'd been expecting earlier.

Something about her empathetic response—and knowing how many of her own memories she brought with her—gave his own grief about the situation permission to finally settle in and make itself at home in his mind and heart.

"I'm truly sorry, Doug. It's hard enough for me, being here with your grandparents gone. I know it's got to be awful for you."

"This is the first time I've been here since

Grandma passed. To tell you the truth, I didn't think it would bother me all that much since she hadn't lived here for a long time. But standing here now, it's…it's a lot. I'm glad I'm not here alone."

He squeezed her hand and let go, not wanting to push his luck on two fronts at once.

"I'm glad I'm not here with a stranger, Quinn. I'm glad it's you."

She smiled again, but this time it was the precise, careful smile he suspected any of her clients would be familiar with.

"I'm just happy I can help. We can go ahead and get started now." She turned and walked inside.

Doug felt like he was with a stranger after all.

Chapter 5

QUINN WALKED STRAIGHT through the kitchen, boots making a faint crackling sound on the dry linoleum. She dodged around the huge rectangular table that still held a sunflower-shaped napkin holder, cheery yellow salt and pepper shakers, and an iridescent tan vase full of desiccated flowers.

She pushed white curtains covered with printed daisies aside, willing the heavy old double-hung window to open instead of jamming. Turning the curved lock proved to be a finger-straining trick, but the solid bottom section rolled up smoothly. Not a single one of the six little panes of glass rattled.

She smiled at the faint thunk of the pulley and weight hidden inside the window's frame adjusting, one of her most-loved old-school technologies that worked better than the modern alternative. Or at least it was more pleasing to use.

Sure enough, the window stayed put right where she left it.

Fresh air streamed in, floating the curtains back

and pushing more of the closed-up staleness away. She put both hands flat on the smooth, white-painted windowsill, and leaned forward until her nose was barely an inch away from the screen.

Quinn wished she could stay there for a while, looking out toward a carefully harvested cornfield. Take a few minutes (maybe a few hours) to catch her breath and get her brain back into gear.

She heard Doug's footsteps as he passed through the kitchen and into the dining room next door, then another window going up.

She had to keep herself from getting too comfortable with him.

Too friendly.

Too hopeful.

For all she knew, Doug had a wife and three kids to get back to in Georgia. Or hell, maybe he was a grandfather himself, just like his cousin. Lots of men didn't wear a wedding ring, so that didn't mean anything.

And there was the very real fact of Quinn's own...*boyfriend* sounded too strange for a man she'd known for a couple of years now. Not to mention coming from a woman in her fifties.

The slow cooling and eventual souring of her relationship with Jeff couldn't be a factor today. Increasingly unappealing or not, the relationship still existed.

And wasn't she getting an absurd number of steps ahead of the situation in even thinking Doug might be an alternative?

Quinn stood up straight, brushing her hands together to clear away the coating of house dust.

If she was really lucky and didn't manage to

make a total fool of herself, maybe she and Doug could at least rekindle their good friendship.

Drive into the closest little town, grab dinner and talk. Figure out who they both were now. Get this melancholy shared task finished up, and move on.

Yes, that made perfect sense.

Assuming she could put how good, how *right*, his hand felt around hers out of her mind.

And how bad she felt when he let go.

She turned to see him standing in the doorway, watching her, and her professional realtor self stepped forward, politely shoving her nervous-kid-self and lonely-woman-self to the side.

"I've shown a lot of older houses with windows like this, but I don't think I've ever seen one where they're so well-maintained. If everything else is in such great condition, you won't have any trouble finding a buyer. If you decide that's what you want."

Doug nodded, his eyes already ranging around the rest of the kitchen. He absently flipped the ancient brown light switch on, then back off once the old-fashioned frosted glass globe in the ceiling lit up.

No doubt lost in a thousand memories that Quinn couldn't afford to indulge in right now.

Right. So, appraisal.

The kitchen was old-farmhouse-typical, meaning square, cut off from the rest of the house, and way too small for modern cooks. Lots of solid wooden cabinets that would no doubt get ripped out first thing. Same with the yellow linoleum counters that matched the walls, even though they were spotless and the strips of metal lining the edges didn't show a speck of rust.

A true aficionado might want to keep the vintage

white porcelain double sink, especially with its wide grooved wings on both sides. Possibly the gorgeous old electric stove that stood out because it was powder blue instead of white.

But Quinn knew a new owner would probably want to rip all of that out along with as many of the beautiful plaster and lath walls as they could. Determined to force a modern aesthetic onto a gorgeous example of previous-century pride and craftsmanship.

She saw it way too often in St. Louis and in farmland Missouri to expect anything different.

"The decision really is up to me and Jenny at this point." Doug ran one hand over the faintly rippled surface of one sunshine yellow wall. "I haven't had time to even glance at the will, but she said something about her being executor and me being backup. She wants us to decide together. I asked her to send a copy to where I'm staying out in Carlyle. Didn't want to show up and distract her with the new baby and all."

Quinn let out a laugh before she could stop herself.

"I'm sorry, I know that lack of sleep thing is no joke. I stayed with Ben to help out when all three of his kids were born. Now two of them have kids of their own."

"I should have asked about Ben, but it sounds like he's doing good. And you're a *great*-aunt now, huh?"

Like every person she knew who was happily child-free but had nieces or nephews, Quinn had an absurd number of child photos on her phone. Along with an irresistible compulsion to show them off, nearly as bad as her friends who had kids of their own.

She crossed the room, tapping the screen to get to the right folder.

"I'm an extremely *proud* great-aunt. In fact, I'm still the cool Auntie Q who got to hear all the questions they wouldn't ask their parents. I hope the next generation will do the same."

Doug had his phone out before she got there, and they traded with a shared giggle that felt more natural than anything else had so far.

Quinn's heart melted (along with a bit of her worry about a wife and/or kids). She was looking at a seemingly endless variety of sweet poses featuring a big goofy yellow mutt of a dog and a regal beauty of a black cat. Including quite a few of them snuggled up together.

"My cheering section," Doug said, his voice soft. "Spoiled-rotten Maya pup and Prince the insufferable cat. These kids are adorable, Auntie Q."

"So are your critters. Where are they now? Do you board them when you're away?"

He glanced at her, a little bit of a blush creeping across his cheeks.

"A friend of mine stays with them. They all know each other, so it's just easier. Getting a cat into a crate isn't my idea of fun."

Instead of feeling a stab of jealousy about this friend who obviously meant a lot to him—a burst of jealousy entirely misplaced in space and time—Quinn only nodded.

She grabbed on to the relief of gaining a little distance like a lifeline.

"No, cats aren't the best at dealing with change. A

roommate of mine had a sweetheart of a tabby, until it came time to go to the vet. Then affectionate, gentle kitty turned into the Tasmanian Devil."

They exchanged phones again, and even the brush of fingers didn't affect her as much as it had before.

"Listen, we have way too much to catch up on," she said. "Carlyle is on the way home for me. Maybe we can grab dinner after we're through here? Then tonight I'll get everything about the house and land written up, and you get a good look at the will. If it works for you, we'll compare notes tomorrow."

The soft, open expression on his face closed up again, and Quinn replayed her words in her mind. Not exactly the most…friendly plan of action, perhaps. But every inch of distance in a situation that could go so wrong, so fast was worth the effort.

Even more so considering her own history with Doug at Carlyle Lake.

She firmly ignored the whisper, probably coming from the softest, least trustworthy depths of her heart.

But what if everything went so right instead?

"Sure, tomorrow should work for me," Doug said. "Tonight does too."

Quinn nodded, ready to get the rest of the walk-through handled so she could get a little time to herself. The drive out to Carlyle would give her a chance to catch her breath, at least.

And she really did want to hear more about Doug's life.

Well, anything more would be an improvement. All she knew was Atlanta, two adorable pets with a mysterious and familiar petsitter, and a cousin with a new grandchild.

"All right, good," she said, trying not to frown at her own small talk. "I'll do everything I can to make this easy for you and your family. Easy as it can be, anyway. Let's get this hardest part over."

Chapter 6

Doug pulled the Jeep into an empty spot at the edge of a graveled parking lot, beside a long building made of rough-hewn logs. Or maybe some other material designed to look that way, since it featured so many big windows and a broad deck overlooking the lake.

Not exactly a typical design feature for a historical building. Either way, the effect was nice.

He couldn't stop wondering if Quinn had decided to make a run for it back to St. Louis after all.

He hoped not, but he'd understand if she did. Despite flashes of comfort between them, most of the house tour/walk down memory lane had been awkward at best.

He turned off the engine, deciding to grab dinner for himself and watch the sun set over the lake even if she didn't make it.

The broad slate-blue expanse of Lake Carlyle in front of him rippled in the early evening breeze. A small flotilla of sailboats glided across the middle, leaving the area nearly silent without the usual company of racing motorboats. Only the wind passing through a line of brilliant orange maples along the road made any noise at all.

The opposite bank's tree line was barely visible in the distance as the lowering sun shaded the whole scene toward pink.

Doug opened the door and stepped out, stretching with both arms over his head before he leaned against the warm hood of the Jeep. The motor ticked and pinged to itself, reminding him as always of an athlete stretching and cooling down after a hard run.

Walking through the rest of his grandparents' house had only gotten harder for him, and he assumed for Quinn, too. He couldn't say even now whether the missing bits of furniture, decorations, and strange little odds and ends that went with her to the assisted living home bothered him more than the way so many things looked like his grandmother had only gone into town to pick up groceries.

Only two places seemed unchanged to his eyes, even after so many years away.

The strangely neat basement, all concrete floor and stone walls and naked light bulbs, down a flight of rock-solid wooden stairs from the kitchen. Only the water heater, furnace, and a few carefully arranged and labeled storage boxes—full of holiday decorations awaiting their turn in a spotlight that would never come again—had ever occupied the huge space.

And the part barn, part garage building outside, as packed full as the basement was empty, but still neatly organized. Aside from enough space to park three cars, the whole thing was divided into separate rooms with their own doors on both levels. All manner of tools for the house and farm and every model of vehicle ever owned by a family member still waited on walls and in drawers inside, clean and ready to use.

And thank goodness, or whatever angels kept thieves or bored kids away, the big porch swing was tucked inside one of the parking spots.

Like so much of the house and the land, dusty but undamaged.

The aroma of something delicious roasting nearby set his stomach to growling, reminding him how long ago breakfast had been back in Tennessee. He vowed to stuff himself silly inside, take himself to the lovely little lakeside cottage that was his for the next week, and go to bed nice and early.

Tomorrow was soon enough for watching his mind go round and round in circles after itself, wondering if he'd ever hear from Quinn Hedges again.

So of course her blue realtor's sedan pulled in beside him then, upsetting his newly made plans and the precarious equilibrium he'd regained on the drive.

Instead of walking around to wait by her door, Doug stayed where he was. Even he could read such clear signs suggesting he back off, slow down, and keep his distance, like a jerk tailgating on the highway.

He waited until Quinn finally stood beside him, taking in her own deep breath.

"I can't remember the last time I was here," she

said. "I forget how beautiful it is. Sorry I took so long. I had to get gas."

Doug looked at her, wondering if that was true or if she'd stopped to debate going home and never looking back. He couldn't read a thing in the way she stared out at the sailboats.

"No worries. This isn't exactly the kind of place that takes reservations. The folks I rented the cottage from insisted it's the best food on the lake."

The wind gusted hard enough to stir up white-caps, and the deepening chill got a shiver out of Doug before he could stop it. Now Quinn smiled at him.

"Weren't you always the one proclaiming you could go out without a coat? No matter how cold it was?"

He grinned and held out one arm toward the restaurant.

"All those years of living in the South. Must have thinned my hearty Midwestern blood, huh?"

"I don't know about that. I can tell you middle age has me turning the heat down a lot more than I turn it up. Just one of the many changes they don't warn you about."

Doug managed to bite back his reply about hearing all about internal temperature changes from the petsitting "friend" he'd mentioned earlier.

He and Mare had parted on good terms. Good enough that he trusted her to keep an eye on his beloved pets, and that she was willing and happy to do it.

He didn't need a textbook to know Quinn wouldn't appreciate hearing all about that right now, no matter how this evening and the rest of the week turned out.

After a quick peek inside the dark wood interior that happened to be full of families with rowdy kids at the moment, they gladly agreed with the waiter's suggestion that they enjoy the peace and quiet out on the deck.

Exactly where Doug had planned to eat on his own. Sharing the view with Quinn could only make the evening better.

Only one other couple sat at the cozy round wooden tables on the wide, weathered-to-gray expanse. Doug and Quinn settled at the opposite end. He didn't mind one bit to be out of the wind, and with a perfect view of the lake and the now-distant sailboats.

"Not the fanciest place for a friendly reunion," he said, smoothing the brown cotton tablecloth, "but the company is good."

"Not bad for the middle of Illinois. What made you decide to stay out here?"

Doug nodded toward the water.

"Georgia is beautiful, and Atlanta has more than its fair share of parks and great architecture. But I don't get out to lakes or the ocean often enough. This seemed like a good neutral location for peace and quiet."

He again kept his thoughts to himself, but he knew Quinn was thinking the same thing. Remembering one of her visits from college, the summer after he graduated high school. As always seemed to happen when they saw each other, they'd ended up together, at least in some sense.

On that visit, *together* included a camping trip to this very lake.

And a weekend full of the best sex of Doug's life, and one of the best weekends of his life altogether. One of the many memories that left him wondering why they'd ever let each other go.

The flush in her cheeks and her sad smile confirmed he wasn't alone in his memories, and maybe not in his wondering.

"Tell me about Atlanta," she said. "I've driven though a couple of times, and got caught in that massive airport longer than I want to remember. What do you get into down there?"

Doug sat back as the waiter brought water for them both, along with a beer for Quinn and hard cider for himself.

"I get into electrical engineering," he said. "For a long, long time. Working with big heating and cooling systems for the last several years."

"You mean for houses?"

He shook his head, wishing he could feel as interested in his recent projects as she sounded.

"More for buildings. Office buildings, convention centers, that kind of thing."

Quinn's eyes widened, the same way Doug's probably did when he first heard about the job.

"That's quite cool. Especially for the guy who was bored with math and had no interest in going to college."

Doug took a long drink of his cider, the dry apple flavor bubbly and crisp in his mouth.

"I think the *key* is I was bored with the math I could get in high school. When I left for Atlanta, I still didn't plan to go to college. I had no idea what I wanted to do, really. I just knew it was an up-and-coming city and I needed to go. I started hanging out with people working in the field is all."

"That's a lot, Doug. You decided to make a change and you did it. A whole lot of people never get that far. Good for you."

He touched his glass to hers. No matter how he felt about his work at the moment, the admiration from her was unambiguous.

And it felt damn good.

"And you," he said. "You got yourself to St. Louis just like you always wanted to, that's fantastic. The last thing I remember you wanting to do was management, right? What got you into real estate?"

Chapter 7

QUINN SAT BACK in her chair, glad the angular wood had sturdy cushions covered in brown fabric that matched the tablecloth. Even the miniature table lamp off to the side of every table had a cute tasseled lampshade in the same color.

There was no point in her back and backside being as uncomfortable as Doug's entirely reasonable question made her feel.

"I got into real estate almost by accident," she said. "I got all the way through earning my MBA, still enjoying what I was studying, looking forward to starting my career. And then I did."

She paused, staring out at the lake. All the lovely sailboats were out of sight now, and a few yellow specks of campfires on the far side stood out. Burning against the gathering purplish dusk over the water.

When she turned back and realized Doug was simply watching her and waiting, Quinn's breath caught. She remembered him struggling to give her the time to think, to consider and choose her words carefully. Always jumping in to fill the gaps, as if he couldn't tolerate the silence.

She had the feeling now that he'd wait all night long for her to decide what she wanted to say.

"The first few years were good. I worked at a pharmaceutical firm, then transferred to property management. Big apartment complexes, single-family homes, a few towers. Nothing big enough that you would have designed the HVAC for them. That's when I got to know a few realtors. Let me ask you a question. What was it about the engineers that inspired you to get into that?"

Doug blinked and a slow smile crossed his face. Quinn hoped he wouldn't say out loud what he'd clearly just noticed.

He'd become a better listener, yes. And maybe *she'd* gotten better at bringing people into the conversation instead of talking while she had the chance, when she could wedge in words of her own away from the more...conversationally demanding members of her family.

"It was the focus they had," he said. "The drive. They were moving toward something, *working* toward it, you know? All I'd been doing until then was trying to get away. I realized I had to make a choice. Did I want to drift along, picking up whatever short-term jobs I could and letting that determine where I was going? Where my life was going? Or did I want to *decide* where I was going, choose a direction, and do what it took to get myself there."

Quinn sighed, trying to keep it to herself. That was one of the many ways she'd attempted to justify their repeated splits over the years.

Doug's lack of drive and her overdrive.

Thankfully she'd managed to identify and understand how her own pursuit of a career that didn't suit her threatened to burn her out before it was too late.

He took a long drink of water, then smiled at her as all the little table lamps on the empty tables around them gradually glowed into soft life at the same time. Try as she might, she couldn't pretend his green eyes weren't every bit as gorgeous as the first time she'd seen them.

"What about being around the realtors got you to make the change?" he said. "That's quite a different career path."

"I used to have all kinds of answers for that, especially to my parents and everyone else who couldn't *believe* I'd worked so hard and decided to give it all up. I'd say I got tired of doing the same thing every day, or I wanted to work for myself instead of someone else. Both true."

She took her turn to sit back while the waiter delivered their salads and a basket full of fresh dark bread that smelled incredible.

"To tell you the truth," she continued, "it was more wanting to be part of people making these big, wonderful changes. Once in a while it's sad, like your grandparents' house or a foreclosure. Most of the time, though, I've been able to help people accomplish this thing they've been working hard for, sometimes for years. That's more satisfying than I could have imagined. Doesn't sound all that different from you wanting to be around people going toward something."

"Not that different at all. I probably would have been a lot better off a couple of times buying a house with you instead of some of the boneheaded decisions I made. Buying a house with your help, I mean."

Quinn smiled at his blush, and the way Doug attacked his salad as if he was defending himself from a bowl of romaine and iceberg lettuce with a few carrots and cherry tomatoes thrown in for color.

Hers looked equally uninspiring, but everything was crisp and delicious, with what might be the best herb vinaigrette she'd ever tasted.

"Well, I might have a colleague or two in Atlanta if you're ready for a change of address," she said, winking. "Tell me about your house, where you live."

"No problems with this address at all. Close to downtown, a gorgeous old tree-lined neighborhood in Decatur. The house is about a hundred years old, with what you realtor types would call character in every square inch. Not a Craftsman bungalow as in it came from the Sears catalog, but that's the style. It's a constant project like any old house. Turns out I enjoy that part of it."

Quinn stopped herself a split-second before asking the typical next questions about good schools and how many bedrooms.

"I hope you have a big fenced-in yard for that sweet dog of yours."

Doug laughed and nodded.

"I do, but Maya refuses to consider it adequate when the weather's nice. There's a dog park about a mile away that suits her much better. I think Prince appreciates time to his feline highness self when we're gone, too. What about you? Did you find yourself a brilliant deal on a fabulous house?"

"I have to admit I did," Quinn said. "You may not

be surprised to hear it's from the same time and similar design as yours, but up here we call it Arts and Crafts. I feel kind of strange saying this to you, but the reason I got such a good price is the owner passed away. His heirs were so happy to get everything settled fast that they didn't say a word about the price. But I was more than fair to them."

Quinn had no idea why she'd felt compelled to add that last bit. She never had before when telling the tale of her amazing bargain house. She didn't think she'd ever told it to someone who was handling the sale of a beloved family home after a death, either.

A family who took her in as one of their own, in some ways more than her own family had.

"Of course you were fair," he said. "I can't imagine you doing anything else."

The admiring look in his eyes sent part of Quinn into panic mode, or at least protection mode. Maybe driven by the part of her that had never really fallen out of love with Doug, but expected to get let down yet again if they went down that familiar road.

Or to be the one to let *him* down, if she was being honest with herself about their history.

Knowing she might regret it but unable to wait any longer, she blurted out the question that had been in the back of her mind since she first recognized him behind the wheel of his Jeep.

"So you're using the word bungalow with your house. As the proud owner of one myself, that tells me it's solid and charming and cozy. Anyone special sharing space with you and your critters?"

Doug raised his chin and shifted sideways in his

chair without looking away from her eyes, but she was sure she felt a chill all the same.

"No. Just me and the dog and the cat, and I suspect they'd both tell you they'd like more space that isn't cluttered up with all my silly human stuff. No one else. Not right now."

Instead of asking like she dreaded, he only waited. His faint, lopsided smile and barely raised eyebrows asked for him.

"Wondering about me and my cozy house, right?"

His smile deepened, but he still didn't say a word.

"No one special," she said, reaching for a slice of the warm bread and the little glass dish full of pats of butter. "No one who lives there. Except you do have me thinking of adopting a couple of dogs."

Doug waited for her to finish before he picked out bread of his own.

"Someone who doesn't live there, then." He focused on spreading the soft butter over his bread. Meticulous as always in making sure it was perfectly even from edge to edge, unlike her gloppy smears. "As long as they make you happy, that's all that matters."

Quinn took a bite of bread on purpose so she wouldn't have to respond to that one right away, letting the slightly sweet bread and lump of salty butter distract her.

Because the only honest answer would be that Jeff made her happy enough.

For now.

Taking her rather inelegant hint (the way Jeff hardly ever did), Doug washed his bread down with the last swallow of his cider.

"With that bit of awkwardness out of the way, anything I need to know about my grandparents' house? I know you have to do more research and all, but do you think everything is okay?"

She finished her beer: the bright hoppy flavor exactly what she needed to clear her throat and adjust her mind.

"Unless there's something strange in the will, or a surprise in the title search, I don't see any problems if you decide to sell. Anyone used to looking at houses that age would be pleasantly surprised how nice it is. The bigger question is how *you* feel about it. You and Jenny. If you're really ready to sell."

He took a deep enough breath that his chest and broad shoulders moved, then took his turn staring out over the lake as he let it out.

Only a trace of fading purple was left in the sky with no clouds to reflect and amplify the light. A few more couples had joined them on the deck, but it was still quiet enough to hear the little waves stirred up by the increasing wind.

Doug rubbed his mouth with one hand, then turned back, slowly shaking his head.

"I was so sure I knew the answer to that question. Yesterday when Jenny called me, all day long on the drive. Even walking through today, mostly. But thinking about it now…"

He leaned forward and stared at her with an intensity that set off familiar explosions all through her middle.

"How about this," he went on. "We switch away from talk about the house and our various exes and anything else that seems iffy tonight. We enjoy our dinner, talk about everything *else* that really matters to us, and pick up the difficult topics tomorrow. Deal?"

He picked up his half-finished glass of water and held it up, with a real smile this time, and more hope than worry in his eyes.

Quinn picked her own water up, touched it to his, and smiled in return.

"Deal. I think that's our food coming out now, so I'll start. Tell me about the best movies, books, and music you want to make sure I know about. And I will definitely do the same."

Chapter 8

THE COTTAGE on Carlyle Lake wasn't anybody's definition of luxury accommodations.

Shiny new hardwood floors that looked suspiciously like laminate, paired with a sofa and loveseat that might be real leather. A fireplace that was too clean to be anything except gas, with an arrangement of logs realistic enough that Doug still had to look twice.

At the back of the compact room—Quinn probably would have deemed it cozy—a remarkably efficient kitchenette waited for the half-hearted culinary efforts he had planned for the week. He could stand in one spot and reach the range, sink, and refrigerator.

Not designed for cooking with a family, or even two people who weren't already pretty cozy themselves, but the sparkling stainless steel and black granite would be a snap to keep clean.

Doug didn't bother checking the downstairs

bedroom with its king bed or the loft with two twins or anything else.

Instead he dropped his little bag of breakfast groceries on the counter, only pausing long enough to tuck his single guy's supply of milk and cottage cheese into the fridge. He retreated into the sitting room long enough to grab a wool throw blanket with a boldly decorated map of Illinois on it.

Everything else could wait.

He walked right through to the tiny deck out back, much newer than the weathered one at the restaurant, turning lights off behind him as he went. The moon was inching toward full, and more than bright enough in the cold, clear sky.

He parked himself in one of the low, perpetually reclined Adirondack chairs, the wooden planks chilly against his skin. Then he hooked the angled footstool over and let out a breath he felt like he'd been holding in all day long.

His inhale brought aromas of the lake's fresh water, someone grilling nearby, and someone indulging in a bit of weed.

Doug laughed under his breath, because of course his brain served up memories of several times when he and Quinn had indulged themselves. Usually with a group of friends out in the woods or along one of the empty back roads all the kids who grew up in farm country seemed to know about.

Only a few times when it was just the two of them.

Even with the moonlight, he could see tiny dots of campfires along the faraway edge of the lake. Far enough that he couldn't hear a thing.

In fact his cottage was isolated enough on this

side of the lake that he couldn't hear much besides the water's restless stirring in the breeze and his own breathing.

How could he possibly be so exhausted, and yet know he had no chance in hell of getting to sleep? All he'd done was take an easy four-hour drive, walk through a house, and have dinner.

Yet every bone and muscle in his body felt achy and sore, as if he had the flu.

He never would have imagined spending time with the person on earth he'd been the most relaxed with, the most comfortable with for years, would hit him like a slog through a Midwestern winter he wasn't used to anymore.

For the first time since he'd developed his habit of escaping to quiet places like this by himself, Doug wished for a noisy party next door. Or at least someone he could overhear talking.

Anything to distract him from all the stirred-up junk and nonsense inside his head.

As if he'd summoned the gods of cellular to come to his rescue, his phone chirped in his pocket. He answered without looking, entirely unsurprised to hear a sweet-as-honey Southern accent that couldn't have been more different than his own flat Midwestern.

"Everything's fine," Mare said, and he could hear her smile. "Your demonic evil cat was doing everything he could to trip me when I was only trying to feed him. Your sweetheart of a gorgeously perfect dog kept herself where she'd catch me as I fell. I'm on the way back there after a grocery store run, because your cupboards are entirely bare of actual human food that doesn't take hours and hours to cook."

"So just another day at the Atlanta-based Linton household. You could learn to cook with something besides the microwave, Mare. Prince loves you *so* much, and all you do is say terrible things about him."

Mare snorted. "No creature who loves me would attempt to murder me like that. To top it all off, you'll be gone for a week. Imagine what kind of state I'll be in after lying dead on your kitchen floor that whole time. How's it going up there? Did you see the house today?"

Doug shivered again, hard enough to make his teeth chatter. He retrieved the blanket from where he'd dropped it on the footstool and spread it over his legs and up to his chest.

"I saw the house. It's in better shape than I expected, but it was tough. A bunch of my grandmother's stuff was shifted around or gone, from when they moved her into assisted living. No vandalism or anything like that to deal with."

"Good. That's never an easy thing. You seem… off. More than tired. From the sound of your voice, I'm guessing you saw Quinn too."

He tilted his head over toward one shoulder, then the other. He wasn't yet sure whether to be glad he'd talked to Mare about all this or not.

"Yeah, she was there. The attorney hadn't warned her that I'd be the one on the walkthrough. So you might say she was startled to see me. Surprised the hell out of me by having dinner with me."

Mare hummed low in her throat. Doug could see her in his mind—rolling her eyes, shaking her head, lips compressed into a thin line.

"I'm sure she was. Startled wouldn't cover it if

one of my exes from thirty years ago showed up in my life. Not that any of them are half the good person you are, of course. But if she had dinner with you it couldn't have been all bad, right?"

Leaning his head back against the chair's cold back, Doug stared up at the moon, barely flattened on one side.

"Not all bad, no. I wouldn't put much stock in my wild daydreams of us getting back together in this lifetime. We might manage to be friends again before it's all said and done. Maybe."

"Hang on, let me get out of the car. Sounds like you have better cell signal than I do, even out there in the middle of nowhere." A rustling noise, then the thud of a door closing. "So, what are you going to do now? Besides take your well-deserved chance to get out of town for a week. Are you going to see her again?"

"Told you, it's flat as a pancake up here, and I'm right beside a huge lake. Cell signal for miles. I don't know what I'm going to do, Mare. She didn't say much about it, but she has some kind of boyfriend or girlfriend or something. Neither one would surprise me, and more power to her. All I know for sure is she's less single than I am."

This time he heard the heavier thud of his front door, followed immediately by the welcoming chorus of a dog and cat he missed very much right then.

"Well, you may not know that for sure," Mare said. "I know I'd be shocked enough to want a little space if I was in her shoes, even if the ghost out of my past was one I very much wanted to see. Don't give up yet, Dougie."

"And you know how much I hate it when you call

me that. We're supposed to at least talk tomorrow, after we both look at the will. If that all seems fine, I just have to talk to my cousin Jenny and decide what we're going to do about the house."

"Thus giving your dearly beloved Quinn a nice commission, which can't hurt her opinion of you."

Doug shook his head even though no one could possibly see him.

"Nope, no commission. The lawyer told me she refused all payment. Wants to handle all of it as a favor to my family. Which she insisted on before she knew I'd be involved, so the lawyer might want to reconfirm."

"I'm still missing the part where everything is as hopeless as you sound. How did dinner go? Did you two glare at each other and spite-eat the whole time?"

Doug laughed, thankful beyond measure that he and Mare had stayed friends. If they'd dated even a week or two longer, he was convinced that would have become impossible.

"We didn't spite-eat, no, but now I'm pretty sure I need to do that with someone. It was…weird but nice? We talked about music and movies and books, and geeky science stuff, and engineering and real estate. Everything but ourselves, I guess."

Mare giggled. "Sorry, that wasn't meant for you. Sweet Prince just sniffed my ear and licked me with his raspy cat tongue. Maya has her head on my leg, staring adoringly with all her might. She's convinced I'll eventually cave and give her all the treats in the world. So what's your plan for tomorrow? And does it include Quinn?"

"Maya knows she can have two of the crunchy

teeth-cleaning kind before bed. If you accidentally sneak in one and *only* one of the small chicken jerky treats before that, she won't tell me about it. I was thinking I might offer to drive over to St. Louis instead of her coming back out here. I haven't been there for years."

"Makes sense to me, as the action of someone trying to be a good friend, and you're a very good friend indeed. You better get to sleep early then instead of staying up and mooning like a lovesick teenager all night long."

Doug managed to lever himself up out of the chair without grunting, blanket draped over his shoulders. He walked out to into the yard and the few steps to the edge of the lake, watching the moonlight playing over the rippling black water.

"I have to stay up long enough to read through the will, at least. Make sure there's nothing strange waiting to gum everything up. I'm sure everything is fine, and the lawyer Jenny hired didn't find any problems. But I did promise to take a closer look."

"Okay then, that's a promise you need to keep. Meanwhile I'm going to dig through your antiquated and rather charming collection of movies and try to find one I haven't already seen."

Maya chimed in with an obvious pay-attention-to-me *woof.*

"Well, I'll look for a movie after a rousing game of tug of war to tire this sweet girl out. Seriously, Doug, make sure you get some sleep. Having to deal with the house or seeing Quinn would be stressful enough. You can't charge headlong into both after spending the whole night staring at the ceiling."

"You're right, and I won't. Thanks, Mare. For everything."

"You're quite welcome, hon. I'm glad to have these furry beasts spoil me rotten for a few days. You take care. Night."

Doug slipped the phone back into his pocket, wondering how cold the lake must be so late in the year. He could do with a good, hard swim, but hypothermia seemed like a very real risk if the night air was hitting him this hard.

Settling down in front of the amazingly realistic gas logs sounded like a much better idea.

And Mare was right. He had to keep his promise to look over the will, if nothing else to make sure he and Jenny could make the right decision with a clear conscience.

He headed back inside to get started.

Chapter 9

QUINN WONDERED how many times she'd traveled this same stretch of highway in her lifetime. The interstate pale gray under her headlights, traffic light and steady all around her. A surprising number of trees alongside for being so close to a major city.

Heading west out of Illinois, watching for the first glimpse of the soaring stainless steel of the Arch in the distance.

Countless times as a kid, of course, mostly in the huge backseats of her parents' typical road-boat cars. Playing silly games with her brother like trying to spot the most vehicles with out-of-state license plates, back before endless versions of vanity plates made that game a lot harder.

Or else all four of them chattering with excitement about whatever got the adults to make the big trip out of state and across the mighty Mississippi. A baseball game, a festival of some kind. Taking visiting family members into the city to see the sights: maybe a trip to the zoo or Six Flags, or the claustrophobic ride in tiny oval elevators to the top of the Arch.

Always with the awareness that they'd be entering a new world with that first glimpse of the remarkable silvery monument to the nation's westward expansion high above the city skyline. Away from the fields and their straight lines and never-changing routines, and into the excitement of the bustling city.

Then the first few absolutely thrilling trips under her own power. Set loose with her own much smaller (and older) set of wheels, mostly free to determine her own destination.

She was pretty sure her parents had gone to their graves believing she snuck off to St. Louis far more often than she actually did.

And of course the scant handful of times she had were with Doug.

Who she'd just spent hours with, completely out of the blue. And it hadn't been as uncomfortable or awful as she might have imagined on a bad day.

Seeing him hadn't been as...exciting as she'd imagined a few times over the years, either.

She turned on the radio, scanning through countless stations until admitting nothing was going to suit her right now. Switching to more music or news with her phone wouldn't do a thing for her restless mind, either.

The idea of being able to stream music and movies right out of the air would have been pure magic to the teenager she'd been. Even more unbelievable than the sleek but stodgy sedan she drove now, equipped with work-approved backup cameras, lane change warnings, and its very own WiFi to help with all that magic data.

Still, for the first time in years, Quinn was tempted to detour back to the sprawling mall and shopping complex on the Illinois border. If she thought there was even the slightest chance of finding any of the music or movies or even the books Doug had mentioned, she very well might have.

She wasn't quite willing to try to at least stream the music on her phone for some strange reason. Maybe an odd throwback to the analog ways of their dating years, when they had to make the trek to that mall or across the river to the city to obtain books or music. And owning a copy of a movie was a rather expensive proposition, even after the launch of those fancy VCR machines.

Getting home into her own space made a lot more sense, even if she did face a restless night of looking up comp homes out in the vast countryside and wondering what might have been.

And keeping herself from slipping over the dangerous edge of contemplating what might be.

On impulse, she used the car's built-in voice command to call her best friends in the city. The hour was nowhere near late enough to worry about waking such reliable night owls.

Sure enough, Jeri picked up on the first ring.

"Are you *finally* back from your venture into the wilds of Illinois?"

"Almost. Rolling that way, haven't caught sight of the Arch just yet. You two up for company? And a story about me coming face to face with my past with no warning whatsoever?"

"Like you even have to ask, especially with a

juicy teaser like that. We're in the backyard by the fire pit if you're up for that. Have you had dinner yet?"

Quinn smiled, wishing she had just a little bit more of the perfectly seared trout even though she was plenty full.

"I did. But I was too stuffed for dessert if you've got anything irresistible just sitting around waiting for a guest to share it with. The fire pit sounds divine."

She heard the scratch of Jeri covering the phone, then the murmur of a quick conversation with her wife.

"Bev informs me we have a dozen frozen cookies left, her spiced chocolate ones that I love so much. I'm mildly offended that she apparently hid them away from me, but is willing to share with you. I'll recover once I've had mine."

"You'll have to fight me for them," Quinn said. "I'll be right there."

She expected her agitated mind to start up again when she ended the call, but got blissful calm instead. Probably saving up for spilling her guts and stuffing her face with cookies, which she would indeed fight Jeri or anyone else for.

Or maybe all the chatter and unrest would come right back full force once she finally decided to make the futile attempt to sleep.

The mental truce held until she parked beside a gorgeous forest green Mid-century Modern house— one low, wide story with a gently peaked roof, deep eaves, and windows all around. The house sat like a huge L on the quiet lot on a hill above the street level, designed to fit in with the old oak trees already there.

Soft boxy lights at knee height showed the way

along the driveway, around the side of the house, and onto a neat stone path into the expansive back yard.

Quinn knew the house as well as her own, inside and out, because she'd helped her dear friends buy it about seven years ago.

The path continued in a gentle curve before it wrapped into a circle, surrounded by similar lights that gradually changed colors. In the middle, a fire pit made of big, angular rocks held a fragrant, crackling blaze.

A tall woman wearing an ankle-length charcoal gray jacket with a wide, flaring skirt was up and out of one of the lounge chairs the second she saw Quinn.

"You didn't have to get up on account of me," Quinn said, even as she gratefully accepted Jeri's hug.

"What nonsense you're talking right now. Get yourself over here this instant and sit. Bev will be out in a minute with enough cookies that we might even be able to share."

Jeri brushed her waves of shiny black hair over one ear and put an arm around Quinn. They'd been friends since college, and lovers for a brief time not long after. The natural, easy return to an even stronger friendship helped form one of the foundations of Quinn's life.

"You sounded pretty out of it on the phone," Jeri said as they walked toward the heat of the fire. "Downright stunned if I'm being honest about it. Exactly what kind of ghost of Quinn's past did you run into?"

Quinn barely got situated in another of the

wooden lounge chairs with her feet toward the delicious warmth when Bev stepped out through the sliding glass door. As compact and economical as Jeri was tall and rangy, skin brown in contrast with Jeri's Irish pale, Bev had firmly made a point of taking over the kitchen as her own domain when the two of them first met.

That confidence extended and blossomed into a wonderful bakery that had been one of the busiest and most-loved in the neighborhood for more than ten years. Bev had arranged to turn the day-to-day operations over to a carefully trained manager several months ago.

But she refused to allow Jeri too many incursions into the kitchen at home, claiming it served an even more important purpose now as the bakery's test kitchen.

A mouth-watering justification for her claim wafted through the air as soon as she set a plate full of golden-brown cookies on a side table that already held smaller plates, cloth napkins, three mugs and a gleaming steel coffee carafe. Aromas of rich chocolate, plenty of butter and vanilla, and the sharp bite of cayenne pepper had Quinn's mouth watering.

Bev leaned down for her own hug, and she smelled every bit as good as the cookies. She'd pulled her mass of curls into a loose knot on top of her head that went along with her blue jeans and a comfortably faded Washington University sweatshirt.

"You get first pick since you're our *guest*," Bev said, batting Jeri's hand away. "And then I understand you have a juicy story to entertain us with on this fine evening. Hope decaf is okay, sweetie."

Quinn retrieved a plate and two of the palm-sized

cookies.

"Decaf is exactly what I need. No doubt I'm already in for a sleepless night, but I shouldn't make it any worse than it has to be. Maybe telling you two all about it will help."

Jeri laughed as she poured steaming mugsful for all three of them.

"Some things never change, and I'm damn glad of it. Especially since we need your special Quinn-variety intrigue and excitement more than ever to liven up our old married lady lives."

Quinn rolled her eyes as she accepted the coffee, wrapping her hand around the warm mug. Not even a year after she and Jeri resumed their friendship, Jeri and Bev had fallen head over heels pretty much at first sight, and never looked back.

She didn't so much envy their domestic bliss as she hoped to someday emulate it.

"I'll do my best to spice things up," she said. "After I spice up my belly with one of these cookies."

She closed her eyes and sighed at the first bite, as she knew she would with every other bite. Still-soft chocolate chips, followed immediately by the fruity heat of the peppers. A sip of smooth, mellow coffee, and she was ready to talk.

"I know Jeri's heard me talk about Doug, my high school flame. Have I spilled my guts to you about him, Bev?"

Bev paused with her mug halfway to her mouth and shook her head.

"Lord yes, I know about him. From you and from Jeri, I'm sure. Heck of a lot more than a flame from what I remember, and not just in high school from what I've heard. You didn't run into *him* today?"

"I surely did. And I'll probably see him at least a couple more times before he rides off back to Georgia."

In between cookies and coffee, Quinn explained how the day had gone, from the last-minute request to help with the house, to her shock at seeing Doug drive up, to the lovely but confusing dinner.

Jeri got up to add more wood to the fire, then squeezed Quinn's shoulders on the way back to her own chair.

"No wonder you sounded so bad when you called. Well, no. Not *bad*, exactly, but jolted, maybe." She was silent, but with her unmistakable mouth-puckered-and-brows-drawn-down expression that meant she wasn't finished. "I've known you long enough that I get to point out how you called us rather than Jeff. I doubt that surprises you any more than it does me."

Quinn slowly shook her head, wishing the coffee was spiked with something. She didn't even want to admit to herself that Jeff hadn't crossed her mind once since she'd halfway told Doug about him.

"I'm not thrilled to admit it never occurred to me to call him until you just said that. But no, I'm not surprised. We've kind of gotten into a dull patch."

Bev rolled her eyes and reached for the last cookie.

"You're not fooling me for one instant, Quinn, and probably not even fooling yourself. He's a very nice guy, but you two started out in a dull patch with occasional comfort sex on the side. I think you've moved on to polite and barely even involved."

"Be honest with me," Jeri said. "Are you two even friends any more? Were you ever?"

Quinn stared up at the sky, tinged with the orange of city lights, then into the fire.

"We never really were, no. Not like with Doug."

Bev patted her arm. "Okay then. This doesn't solve what you're going to do about *him*. But I think you've known for a while now that you're just marking time with Jeff, or without him. Maybe putting that to a merciful end will help clear your head for figuring out the rest."

And because cell phones were infernal devices of torment and rotten timing, Quinn's chirped in her pocket.

"Oh, that has to be a sign from somebody about something," Jeri said, giggling and sitting forward. "I'm placing my bet on that being Doug. Either pining for our dear Quinn, or angling to see her tomorrow."

"I think you're probably right," Bev said with a scowl. "But I'll place my marker on poor, fading out of the picture Jeff. Got a twinge that he's about to be evicted from the tiny little sliver of Quinn's heart that he managed to occupy."

Quinn pulled the phone out, putting it upside down on her thigh. "Either of you going to tell me what you win?"

Bev shook her head. "Not a chance. That's private."

"I might be persuaded," Jeri said, reaching for the phone.

Quinn batted her hand away, much like Bev had when Jeri was after the cookies. Her heart fluttered like a silly kid with a crush when she held the phone up.

"Well, get ready to pay up, Bev. This is Mystery

Man from the Past himself. And I quote, 'Really sorry to bother you so late, hope you sleep right through this. Something strange in the will after all. We'll need to go back out to the house. By the way, good morning. Your choice for breakfast if you want, but my treat.' "

Both Jeri and Bev erupted into a schoolgirl chorus of high-pitched *oooooooohs*.

"There goes our company for the night," Jeri said. "Look how fast she's packing up to leave. I would have known it wasn't from Jeff if you hadn't said a word, my dear."

Quinn was indeed sitting up, returning her plate and mug to the little end table.

"Will it make any difference if I remind you that's essentially a work text? Since I *am* his realtor?"

Jeri got to her feet, shaking her head, and pulled Bev up beside her. They each grabbed one of Quinn's hands and stood her up between them.

"That might work," Bev said, "if either one of us ever saw you interrupt yourself *for* work at this hour. Ever. Seriously, though, you need to at least try to get yourself some sleep. Sounds like you're in for an interesting day tomorrow no matter what happens to turn up in that will."

Rather than pretend to argue, Quinn stepped forward into the group hug she needed very badly in that moment.

"You're right," she said. "I at least need to go through the motions. Thank you for listening to me. And even more for the spectacular cookies."

"Thank you for the excuse to eat them," Jeri said. "You know you're welcome any time. As long as you give up the gossip. Night, hon."

Chapter 10

DOUG SAT on the front porch of his grandparents' house, feet on the pebbly concrete sidewalk, knees not quite up to his shoulders. Lost in memories of sitting exactly there when his feet dangled without touching the ground at all.

The sun had barely risen high enough to peek over the house, casting long, deep blue shadows on the weedy mess in front of him. From the looks of the slate gray sky and the cool, damp feel of the breeze, yesterday's bright sunshine wouldn't be appearing.

The thought of how his grandfather would have reacted to the grass getting into this kind of shape was enough to make Doug shiver. Almost enough to send him scurrying over to the barn to try to get the ancient weed-eater and lawnmower going.

He sipped from the small thermos he always traveled with, wishing he'd thought to bring his own coffee from home as well. The stock at the cabin was energizing to be sure. But it needed a good bit more creamer and sugar than he was used to.

At least he'd had his usual Grape Nuts and cottage cheese to give himself a routine and a bit of much-needed equilibrium, knowing he'd be seeing Quinn today.

Who'd politely but firmly refused his offer of breakfast in favor of lunch later on. Her reasoning of wanting to get the will sorted early in the day if they could made perfect sense.

And her words still felt as chilly to him as the early morning air.

He'd already wandered around the outside of the house enough to get his jeans wet all around the bottom, almost up to the knees. The simple fact that he no longer had a key hadn't occurred to him until he arrived an hour ago.

No wonder, really, after an even more restless night than he usually had sleeping in a strange place.

It wasn't the comfortable bed, or the cool bedroom air, or the sound of the lake outside the window. If the nearly fifty years of his life until last night were any indication, he should have slept like a stone. Especially after a drive and a stressful day.

All the restlessness came from inside his own mind, and his own heart.

He was about to get out his phone to check for a message from Quinn when he spotted a dust trail in the distance.

Doug stood, brushing dust from his backside, laughing under his breath at himself.

Why on earth did he have the same sense of shy awkwardness he sometimes felt after having sex with someone for the first time?

Not that he hadn't made love with Quinn, countless times over several years. The one thing that never failed to work between them, no matter what else fell out of balance.

Yesterday all they'd done was talk and shake hands. Not so much as a hug. Still, he wrestled with uncertainty of what to do when she arrived.

Shake her hand again? Move in for a hug, and maybe give the rotten impression that he felt entitled to touching her? Hang back and let her decide, at the risk of appearing cold and uncaring? That seemed to be his default, and it rarely worked out all that well.

Rather than the blue sedan with a rather bright logo on the door for her business, today Quinn drove a sporty dark green two-door. Doug was willing to bet she'd made the drive out from St. Louis quite a bit faster, and had a hell of a lot more fun doing it.

He strolled toward the driveway as she parked and climbed out of the low-slung car, unable to hide his grin.

"That car is absolutely perfect for you, Quinn. I love it."

She grinned back, and a huge part of the tension Doug had been worried about evaporated. As was often the case, his honest response had been the right one.

Maybe he'd finally remember that lesson next time.

"Why *thank* you," she said with a perfect curtsey. "I treated myself for my fiftieth, after working my ass off for a few years to make sure I could afford it. I figured getting through half a century was the ideal time to give my natural-born lead foot the engine it's always deserved."

"You earned it through years and years of high-speed practice, I'd say. Makes me feel a little less guilty about you having to drive all the way back out here today."

She waved one hand and shook her head, and thank goodness she was still smiling. She wore a charcoal gray hoodie to go with a red t-shirt and blue jeans, and every bit of it suited her as well as the car did.

"Not a problem, I don't mind at all. You'd have to work awfully hard to be the toughest client I've dealt with. Trust me. Honestly, I'm more curious than anything. How could neither of us have known about a sub-basement here?"

Doug shook his head and shrugged. "No one ever said a word to me. You can look at the will if you like, of course."

Quinn walked toward the side door, keys already in her hand.

"I still have a copy, remember? And the pictures you sent were clear enough for a strange situation. 'Take special care in sub-basement' speaks for itself, don't you think? Hey, how'd your fur kids do overnight without you? Don't even try to tell me you didn't check in."

Doug held up both hands as he stepped up onto the porch beside her. He hesitated to even think it to himself, but so far this was much closer to the reunion he'd imagined so many times over the years.

All they were missing was the hug.

"I did check in, yes. They're fine. Any time I'm out of town, they know they'll get spoiled stinking rotten no matter where they stay. So they don't mind all that much."

"Smart man." She opened the door and paused

for a second, then nodded. "Nowhere near as bad inside today. Hopefully this won't take us too long."

Stepping into the kitchen behind her and closing the door, Doug couldn't help wishing it did take a good long time, as long as neither of them got hurt or anything like that.

Once this was finished, there wouldn't be a reason he and Quinn *had* to spend time together. He could hope she'd want to, and he certainly did want to. But she'd be entirely justified in shaking his hand again and walking away.

Maybe walking back to the person who she hadn't quite told him about the day before, and who didn't live in her house.

Beside the doorway through to the sitting room waited a small wooden door painted the same cheery yellow as the walls. Even the dark metal doorknob was smaller than in the rest of the house, and kind of an oblong shape as well.

A simple hook-and-eye latch fastened the door at his shoulder height, with a darker arc of paint where the curved hook swung free when it was open. Not too tall for his grandparents to reach, but too high for kids to accidentally open the door and tumble down those stairs.

"Basements usually creep me out," Quinn said, smiling back at him over her shoulder as she flipped the light switch to the right and started down the steps. "But this one never did. Too clean and too well-lit, I suppose."

"You would not have liked the one in my first house in Atlanta. Not when I first moved in, anyway. It wasn't much more than a room dug out of the clay, for one thing. Big enough to hold the furnace and water heater. On top of that, someone left a whole bunch of stuffed animals down there. Well, not stuffed, they were taxidermy. Arranged all over the place, but every one staring at the basement door."

Quinn walked far enough out on the concrete floor to give him room before she turned with her hands on her hips. Her scowl was far more amused and adorable than threatening.

"You did *not* just tell me that when I'm standing in a basement, un-creepy or not. And with some unknown room we're supposed to take care in hidden under our feet."

Doug managed a casual wink. "Sorry about that. You knew my grandparents. They were a lot more likely to hoard actual stuffed animals rather than anything that used to be alive."

He turned in a slow circle, trying to actually examine walls made of carefully stacked and mortared stone as if he hadn't seen them his entire life.

"I can guess all day long about whatever they might have been keeping down here," he said. "But I don't have a clue where to look for where they may have hidden the door."

Quinn walked around the edge of the basement, staring at the floor.

"It may not be a door like you expect. It could be set into the wall, or hidden underneath something else, especially if they kept it a secret from a bunch of curious grandchildren. Maybe even from your parents and aunts and uncles. I've had a couple of buyers stumble across things like that, and the previous family who lived in the houses had no idea."

Doug took the clue and headed toward the furnace close to one wall, by far the biggest thing in the whole room. He'd intensely disliked the huge, hulking oil model that stood here when he was a kid.

Besides the black, sooty bulk of it, he never managed to not jump at the low, thumping boom it gave out every time it fired up.

The current, much smaller version ran on gas, like the one in his house back in Georgia. Only about as tall as his shoulders, and the light gray still visible after over a decade.

He stood beside it, phone out with the light on high, following two parallel lines in the concrete. They came from the rock wall at a right angle toward the furnace, about three feet apart.

"This might be… I don't know, it might be just the way they had to put the gas lines in or something."

He knew Quinn was beside him by the scent of her skin and some sort of earthy perfume she wore, cutting through the dusty basement smell.

"They could be," she said, touching one of the grooves with her boot toe. "Strange how they only run from the wall to the front of the furnace, though, not any further out into the room. And the gas lines come in from overhead."

She pointed without looking up, and sure enough, black steel pipe ran alongside one of the thick wooden beams a few inches above his head.

Okay, not the best display of his powers of observation or logic, even considering Quinn's years of realtor experience, or the walkthrough the day before.

Time to put his engineering skills to work.

"Assuming we're not looking at an old repair or

something equally mundane," he said, "and this is honestly a secret passage, there must be a way to open it."

He moved his light to the metal body of the furnace, and along the beams that supported the ceiling of the basement. Looking for a cleverly hidden switch, or maybe a knob.

He suspected Quinn was looking for the same along the flat rocks of the walls.

Doug made it all the way around the furnace at the same time she finished her examination.

Just as they stood side by side, the furnace gave its milder version of the start up boom.

Which turned out to be quite impressive and more than a little frightening when standing right next to it.

Quinn grabbed Doug's arm at the same time he grabbed for his chest, where his heart threatened to pound itself right out.

"Wow, hope I look a hell of a lot braver than I feel right now," she said.

But she didn't let go.

"Yeah, not feeling especially courageous right now myself. At least we know it works, huh? No problems at all after no one living here for a while."

She laughed and squeezed his arm before she stepped away.

"I'll be sure to make a note of that. See anything that might look like a switch or trigger?"

Doug's eyes went to a vertical support beam on his side of the furnace: a solid four-by-four hunk of wood that looked sturdy enough to hold up the whole house by itself. He couldn't see any wires or conduit.

But the same kind of old-fashioned brown light switches that were throughout the house sat on the side of the beam closest to the wall. Old enough that it had two push buttons rather than anything close to modern.

Where no one could see it unless they walked back here like he and Quinn just had.

If they happened to look higher than any sort of switch should have been. Almost to his shoulder height, just like the latch on the door in the kitchen.

And only if they had a light of some kind. Because it was deep in the shadow cast by the body of the furnace itself, and would have been with the older model, too.

"It couldn't be that simple," he whispered.

Chapter 11

Quinn did her best not to shudder when Doug stepped closer to the furnace.

As far as she was concerned, having to spend even brief time next to so many of them was by far the worst part of her job. Even in a basement that had never bothered her otherwise.

She'd mentioned it to her father once, that deep-seated fear that she couldn't seem to leave behind, even though she dealt with it so often. He'd told her about a visit to family over in Indiana, people she didn't remember at all. Apparently they were close relations around the time she was born.

Good people, too, to hear her dad talk about them. Real shame when they passed away, and he missed them still.

Despite the fact that they apparently left the door to the little shed that held their ancient old coal-burning furnace unlocked.

Even when toddlers were around.

Apparently their own kids had grown up in the

house and had no problems at all, so it never occurred to them.

Not until after a not-quite-two-years-old Quinn—playing outside and deliriously happy to be moving under her own power—toddled into the furnace room. Curious as she still was today, but nowhere near so steady on her feet.

Turned out focusing on the pretty little black rocks scattered across the floor at that age had been too much for her motor skills.

Sending her stumbling into the hot furnace hands-first.

Quinn reflexively clenched her fists, thankful as she'd ever been that no permanent damage had been done to her hands.

Only to her so far lifelong inability to be comfortable around any sort of furnace. Even a fairly new and much less intimidating gas model like this.

When Doug shone his phone light along a thick support beam, she couldn't help stepping closer herself.

She'd seen plenty of similar switches, sometimes on the units themselves, sometimes on a nearby wall or support like this. In fact, she'd already located both the electric switch and the gas switch for this unit on their inspection yesterday.

Both on the other side from where they were standing.

The beam also had no evidence of wires of any kind, or even scars or discoloration in the wood from where they might have run before. Drilling out such a huge piece of wood to hide wires in a basement of all places didn't make much sense, either.

He whispered something she couldn't hear over

the furnace's mild rumble, then looked at her, eyebrows raised.

"Should I try it? See if it opens the secret passage?"

"Well, since I spotted the actual furnace controls yesterday, I'd say odds are high it does something else. Assuming it does anything at all."

He leaned closer to her, and she was breathlessly certain he was going to kiss her. Not anything passionate, mind you, or even over some kind of bright, obvious line for two people who'd so often been intimate in the past.

Even a peck on the cheek would hit her like a runaway freight train in a tense moment like this. And after the long, long night she'd spent thinking over what felt like every single moment in their recurring relationship.

Instead he winked. "Very observant of you, as always. I didn't notice those at all. So here goes. Might want to stand back if you suspect it might be *literally* under our feet."

Quinn did take a step back, and smiled at herself for holding her breath.

Doug pushed the bottom button in and stepped back beside her.

And nothing happened.

He leaned forward again, pushing the top one, then the bottom one again.

When he turned back to her, he looked like a crestfallen little boy, glinting silver in his beard and all.

"Listen, if it really is some kind of secret," she said, "it wouldn't be obvious and easy to find, right? Can you think of anywhere your family might have hidden a hint like that? I can't imagine the will would mention a sub-basement if there isn't one. Or without some way to find it."

"Not really. Not unless there's something else in the will both of us missed. I have my copy in the car if you think we should take a look."

Quinn touched his arm without thinking, then felt too self-conscious to yank her hand back. That and too unwilling to hurt his feelings.

"I have my copy too, and the other house paperwork. Go upstairs with me and see what we can find? I brought coffee and a treat."

He covered her hand with his for a second, then nodded.

"All you had to say was coffee. What I had this morning was plentiful and not very good."

She followed him up the stairs, trying her best not to stare at the way his ass and legs moved in his blue jeans. She wasn't sure whether he still biked or not, but from this rather flattering angle, he very much looked like he did.

The two of them had set out on their sturdy thick-tired bikes for this house when she was still in high school, in July, without checking the forecast. By the time they'd arrived, both of them had finished all the water they'd brought and gone begging for more.

Neither of them had any idea it was well over one-hundred degrees that day.

He turned at the top of the stairs, and Quinn had a sinking, thrilling certainty that he knew where she'd been looking. His confident smile turned up the thrill considerably.

"Do you remember sitting in this kitchen," she

said, hoping to cover her blush, "guzzling water like thirsty dogs one overly hot summer day?"

Doug threw back his head and laughed, the wonderful big, deep laugh he hardly ever cut loose with, and every second of the years since they'd seen each other finally fell away.

Quinn might have been seventeen or nineteen or twenty-one again, with no clue of how her life would go. Or any real suspicion that Doug wouldn't always be part of it.

"Of course I remember. It's a wonder both of us didn't throw all that water right back up." He held up his left arm, the back of his hand toward her so his sleek black smart watch showed. "And that may be why I was not only an early adaptor of weather forecasting apps, but I also have an abnormal number of them set to alert me about changes."

"Quite sensible of you." Quinn tapped her own purple watch, then opened the kitchen door. "My own weather watching habit has kept me better prepared than the people I routinely save from rain or hail or snow would ever admit."

In fact, the morning had turned quite a bit cooler while they were inside, though no rain was predicted until later that afternoon. Even more incentive to get this wrapped up and get back to the city.

Both of them took in a lungful of the fresh, earthy scent of an incoming storm, and shared another smile that set Quinn's belly looping and her heart into overdrive.

They parted ways to go to each of their cars, and Quinn took the chance to breathe deep a few more times. And to remind herself she wasn't here to fall into Doug's arms yet again.

That was all well and good thirty years ago, when she was unsure of who she was and what she wanted.

She gathered up the unusually thick blue folder for this job (that's what it was, after all, a *job*), and kept a harsh laugh to herself.

Jeri might not have meant to the night before, but by mentioning Jeff, she'd reminded Quinn of just how much she wasn't sure what she wanted right now.

Never mind that he didn't seem all that invested in whatever they had going on either.

It seemed that suited Quinn just fine.

Maybe things hadn't changed so much after all.

She backed up and turned, nearly colliding with Doug. Who caught her arms quite neatly when she tried to back up and tripped over her own damn feet.

"I'm sorry," he said, choking back a laugh. "I didn't mean to… Anyway, I thought you might need help. With the coffee and all."

Quinn looked up into his eyes, brilliant green even in the overcast light. Much too close to her own eyes and her burning cheeks.

She pushed the thick folder against his chest with an exasperated sigh.

"I almost forgot about the coffee. Which only goes to show how much I need it. Meet you on the porch?"

He nodded, then jerked his chin that way.

"Already got my copy of the will waiting for us."

This time she walked around to the far side of the car away from the house, where she hopefully wouldn't be surprised by anyone walking up behind her. Not that he'd been especially sneaky or quiet.

When she thought back, she actually had heard his feet crunching on the gravels. She'd simply been too preoccupied with her own catalog of insecure thoughts to pay attention.

Her two stainless-steel travel mugs fit perfectly into the distinctive to-go tray, with dark green cardboard decorated with leaves folded over into a clever box on the other side. Enough high-calorie, higher-satisfaction goodness from her favorite bakery was packed inside to easily balance the heavy mugs.

She was surprised to see Doug hadn't opened her folder. He sat not far from where the porch swing used to hang, legs crossed underneath him like a kid. From the quick way he looked toward the road, she'd just caught him watching her just as boldly as she'd watched him walk up the stairs.

Quinn decided to call that balancing the scales between them, and headed that way.

"What decadent treasure are you bringing me?" he said, leaning forward with his elbows on his knees. "Did you actually brew the coffee yourself?"

She handed him one of the mugs as she sat beside him.

"I didn't brew this, no. But I do make a mean cold brew. All of this is from the best bakery in the city as far as I'm concerned. You have your choice."

She put her own mug on the dusty boards and flipped open the box. Inside sat two squares of flat, sparkly golden-brown cake on little paper circles, a big morning glory muffin studded with sunflower seeds and cranberries, and a carrot cake cupcake loaded down with barely sweet cream cheese frosting.

It was Quinn's turn to laugh at how Doug's jaw dropped and his eyes got wide.

"You brought me gooey butter cake?"

"I figured that would be the perfect way to welcome you back after so many years away. One of my best friends owns a bakery that makes the best in town. Don't worry, there's plenty of other stuff to choose from if your system isn't up for that much sugar and butter any more. Or I can save all of it for clients."

She pretended to move the box away and he grabbed her wrist, his hand warm against her cool skin.

"I think I'll take my chances." He picked up one piece of the cake and raised his eyebrows. "I'm assuming you didn't mean for me to take both of them?"

Quinn pushed his shoulder with her own as she retrieved her own cake.

"I guess I wouldn't fight you for it, since I can get this any time I want. But yeah, I mean to eat this one myself. There are napkins in the box."

"Good. My mouth is already watering enough to need them."

Quinn picked up her own piece of cake, not much more than an inch tall and heavy for its not-quite-palm size. Her teeth crunched through the sugary crust into the namesake gooey top layer, and intense sweetness and rich butter burst over all her taste buds.

Instead of closing her eyes with pleasure, she turned to watch Doug. His reaction didn't disappoint. His eyes rolled closed, and he sighed and slumped toward her.

"Either I've been away too damn long, or this is the best one I've ever tasted. I hope that coffee is strong enough to counteract the sugar crash that's going to hit us later."

"It's pretty high-test stuff. Bev knows to pour mine from her own supply, not what she makes for the amateurs. She offered to pack a whole gooey butter cake for you to take back to Atlanta."

Doug let out a soft laugh around his second bite. He paused again to savor it, letting out a low groan that Quinn tried to pretend she didn't recognize from other pleasurable moments for him.

All these years later, and she still remembered.

"So this Bev knows enough about me to expect I'd want more of this decadent ambrosia, *and* that I'll be heading back to Atlanta?"

Quinn turned her face away to hide her amused scowl. She'd said way too much without thinking right there, and no real way to back out of it, either.

The sugar must already be hitting her brain.

"Well, yeah, I stopped by her house last night on the way home. They were asking what brought me all the way out here, since I did get in kind of late compared to a regular work day."

He nodded, edges of his mouth turned down in a mock frown.

"Got it. Only being polite, huh?"

"That's right. What, you didn't tell your pet-sitting friend how your day went when you checked in last night?"

For a quick second, Quinn had a gut-clenching certainty that she'd said too much. Stepped over the line from teasing into outright rude. But Doug only glanced her way and grinned as he went for the coffee and took a sip.

"Of course I did. Like I said, only being polite. Please be sure to give your friend my most sincere compliments when you're being polite this evening, will you? This coffee is *almost* as good as the cake."

"I will. As long as you mention who brought the cake when you're back down South and singing its praises."

She picked up her travel mug, holding it out until he gave it a solid tap with his.

"You got it," he said. "Thank you for the delicious and remarkably unhealthy treat. I suppose we should try to solve the mystery of the sub-basement while we're at peak sugar and caffeine buzz."

With the last bite of her cake, Quinn allowed herself a full eyes-closed and sigh reaction. Yes, the ultimate St. Louis culinary indulgence was far too sweet and rich to eat every day, or maybe even once a week. But she never failed to savor every bite when she did indulge.

She wasn't the least bit surprised to catch Doug watching her when she leaned over to grab her paperwork folder. She wasn't the only one remembering closer times between them.

And probably not the only one unsure what to do about that.

"I think you have all the same things I do when it comes to the will," she said. "I did find an envelope with the real estate stuff this morning, tucked in with the background paperwork. I'm sorry, Doug, I didn't get a chance to look through everything in advance like I normally would. It's for you and Jenny."

She held out a small, sky blue envelope, about the

size of the old-school thank you notes she hardly every saw any more.

"You didn't get much of a chance to prepare for this whole thing, did you?" He flashed a warm half-smile. "I appreciate you taking everything on at the last minute too much to need an apology. That and getting to see you again."

He took the envelope, and his eyes and his smile took on a sadness deep enough to make Quinn's heart ache. Doug didn't have to say a word to confirm what she'd suspected when she pulled the envelope out of the stack of yellowing, age-crackly papers that morning while she waited for Bev to pack up their treats.

The names on the front were written in his grand-mother's hand.

Chapter 12

DOUG HELD the tiny envelope with the tips of his fingers, trying to convince himself he didn't smell his grandmother's perfume, or the last batch of cookies or loaf of fresh bread she made.

Not nearly as hard as he was trying not to cry in front of Quinn.

So strange that a series of looping, backward-slanted blue ink marks forming his name could yank him out of his middle-aged life and push him back to being a kid again.

He turned it over and slipped the envelope flap loose, thankful his Grandma hadn't sealed it. Ripping a gift like this would have broken his already aching heart.

He glanced at Quinn, wondering for a quick second whether she'd read the folded cream-colored paper inside before giving it to him. Her soft smile reminded him who he was dealing with.

Of course she hadn't. And he was glad a thousand times over she was with him instead of some anonymous person he'd never met until the day before.

He pulled the thick paper out and unfolded it.

My Dearest,

I'm not sure which one of my two wonderful grandbabies will be reading this, so I won't name names. I will say thank you, thank you, thank you for taking care of the things that are left behind.

Your Grampa and I did everything to make this as easy as it could be. Easy as a thing like this can be. The will lets you do what you need to. I hope one of you or someone else in the family chooses to stay in the house, but we both understand if that doesn't happen.

We truly do.

Times have changed, and the last thing either one of us would ever want is for any of you to feel burdened with something like a house no one wants or needs.

The only thing that's not in the will or anywhere else is what you'll find in the sub-basement. I'm sorry I didn't get a chance to tell any of you about it before now.

If you're reading this, my sweet Jenny, I also have to apologize that what you find down there is for Doug. That's a decision that was long out of my hands, possibly since before I was born.

I always thought I'd have more time, and after I left home, I always thought I'd be going back.

That's something you should remember about your life. You will eventually do everything for the last time. Often before you realize it.

The family that settled our land and built our house survived horrible storms that year. So they didn't feel safe enough with a normal basement. My great-grandfather, grandmother, and I have used it for our own purposes.

I have no idea why the treasure within skipped your

parents, only that some treasures follow their own secret rules.

To get down there, look for the light switch behind the furnace. My mother made sure it was out of the little ones' reach when she had it put in. The old way was too dangerous.

No riddles here except the one that amused her and me at the time.

Hold both buttons.

You'll figure it out from there.

Whoever is reading this, I love you. I miss you.

I know you'll make the right decisions, because you always do.

Gramma

Doug closed his eyes, only then noticing he'd cried after all.

He held the pages toward Quinn, leaning into her touch when she rubbed his arm.

"I read it when you did. I heard her voice with every word."

He turned toward her just in time to catch her wiping away a few tears of her own.

"She always did like you," he said. "From the first second she met you."

"I liked her too. And I think she's right. You and Jenny will know what to do about the house, and you with whatever is down there. I'll help as much as I'm able."

Doug nodded, rubbing his mouth. Sitting right here, especially with Quinn, he couldn't imagine watching this house pass out of his family's hands.

But he couldn't imagine living here, either.

He *could* imagine kissing Quinn right now. The

slightest lean toward her would make his intentions clear.

Much as he wanted to, he wasn't sure either of them was ready to cross that line.

"I guess I need to make sure Jenny sees this letter," he said. "And whatever we find down there, new grandbaby or not. Even if I'm supposed to deal with it. Help me check it out?"

"Of course. Now I really want to see what's down there. I hope you'll take the muffin and cupcake. You won't regret it."

He stood, gathering up the clever little cardboard box and his copy of the will.

"If they're half as good as that cake, I'd be a fool not to. Let's get everything else in case the rain gets here early."

A few quick minutes later, they stood on either side of the odd grooves in the concrete floor, tears replaced with excitement.

"Ready?" he said, fingers over both of the round buttons.

Her grin wound him up even more, like it always had.

"Ready to jump out of here if anything too strange happens."

Doug was surprised at a strong flutter of nerves in his chest and stomach. He'd seen too many horror movies, probably.

His beloved Grandma would never put him into danger.

Right?

"You'll have to race me up the steps." He pushed the buttons down at the same time.

For a second that felt like an eternity, nothing

happened.

Then a slow, deep grind started up from under the furnace. Quinn's face paled, and she stepped closer to the stairs.

"Have I ever told you how much I truly dislike furnaces?" she said, raising her trembling voice over the noise. "More like I'm horribly afraid of them, if you want to know the truth."

Doug moved toward her at once, determined to do whatever it took to make the fear in her eyes and voice go away. He no longer gave a damn about lines they should or shouldn't cross.

If he had it in his power to comfort her, he would move the furnace or the house itself or anything else to do it.

But just then the floor under his feet shifted sideways.

Quinn shouted and reached toward him at the same time.

"Watch out!"

He managed an awkward, twisted step, and she yanked him the rest of the way.

After so many daydreams and night dreams, he barely noticed when she put her arm around his waist as his went around her shoulders.

Because the floor was opening up right in front of them.

"It might…" She covered her nose and mouth with her free hand.

Doug did the same and pulled them both a step back. But the air only smelled sort of damp and cool. Cavelike, rather than the awful stink the upstairs had yesterday.

The concrete slab slowly slid under the furnace

with a gritty, rock-against-rock noise. One stone step was visible, then another, heading down into the darkness away from them.

"It's going right under the furnace," Doug said. "But how? If it's been here that long, it has to pre-date electricity."

"Maybe it used to be a pulley? Or a hand crank? I bet we'll see the mechanism when we get down there."

Her voice no longer held a trace of fear. Only excitement that matched the thrilling little bursts of energy going off all over Doug's mind and body.

He looked down at her, needing to see the light of that excitement in her eyes.

He was entirely unprepared when she leaned up and kissed him full on the mouth.

Before he could respond to the titanic explosion her lips set off inside him—perhaps by pulling her hard against him and kissing her back for a good long while, to hell with the mystery room at their feet —she had her cell phone out and aimed the light down.

"They were lucky to have a building site without much groundwater. Otherwise it would have been a constant struggle to keep them both dry. I'd bet we'll find the well is really deep and clean once I get it inspected."

"I…yeah, that may be. You're probably right."

Quinn stepped away from him as the opening got big enough to let them walk down, leaning forward and peering into the opening.

Seemingly unaware of how hard her kiss had thrown him.

While he was still trying to deal with a heart pounding so hard he was dizzy.

"We may have to get a bigger flashlight," she said. "Unless there's light down there too." She finally turned back and looked at him, with her eyes and face lit up more than he'd expected.

He shook his head and smiled, not wanting her to see how much she shook him up if she wasn't feeling the same way.

"I'd be amazed if there's not some kind of light," he said. "This is a family who insisted on having light switches at every door to a room long before that was cool. Official education or not, I'm nowhere near the first with a brain tuned to engineering."

Slab fully retracted, the grinding noise finally stopped, leaving Doug's ears echoing in the silence. He saw four steps now that looked like they were carved out of the bedrock itself before the darkness took over.

Quinn stared at him for a second, then entirely misunderstood his disorientation.

Or at least she pretended to.

"I'm sorry, look at me rushing ahead of you like I have any kind of right to go first. This is your family house."

Doug got out his own phone, thumbing the light on, and decided to go along with the pretense.

"I was just wondering what would happen if that floor slab got triggered by accident. I'm really hoping there's a switch under there to open it, or maybe some way to lock it out."

Quinn stared at him again, and they both burst into laughter. He couldn't quite get his brain to settle on what was so funny, but he was relieved at the shift in focus.

"Now that was spoken like a natural engineer!" she said. "If they used it for a storm shelter even a hundred years ago or more, there has to be something like that, right?"

"I'm sure there is. Actually, look at the switches. Both are still down. That tells me something else makes everything reverse."

"Okay then. After you, my friend."

She held out one arm toward the newly revealed stairs and smiled. Doug stepped forward, determined to continue keeping his feelings to himself.

No matter what that kiss meant to Quinn in the moment, her calling him "my friend" didn't exactly inspire confidence to try it again.

One hand on the rough rock wall to his right, phone light casting ahead, he descended into the sub-basement he'd never suspected could exist less than twenty-four hours ago.

Chapter 13

QUINN WATCHED Doug walk carefully down the steps into the sub-basement, wishing she'd gone on ahead of him after all. Unlike her gut-clenching fear when she thought the furnace was grinding itself into jagged, soon-to-be-airborne pieces, now she was nothing but eager to get down there and check it out.

The only thing she wished for more was that she hadn't slipped up and kissed him like that.

Sometimes getting entirely too close and comfortable with an old friend and former lover was not at all a good thing. Even if getting that close to Doug felt as natural as breathing.

And if the touch of his lips against hers had fired up parts of her she thought died out with her early twenties.

He paused to shine his phone's light around the top of the opening in the floor, then reached to his right.

Several yellowish lights came to life down there,

with a couple of decidedly old-fashioned ticking and popping noises.

Doug turned and grinned up at her.

"I knew it would be sensibly designed. Come on down, these stairs are solid rock, and no water in sight."

He took several quick steps and disappeared.

Quinn glanced at the quiet furnace, then up at the two depressed light switches.

Her memory of Doug's grandmother wasn't only full of welcome and easy affection. Cora Linton had also been entirely practical and as steady as the Mississippi River.

She breathed in the cooler air under her feet, and pushed away her fears of getting trapped two levels underground, in a secret sub-basement, in a long-empty house in the middle of vast Illinois farmland fields.

After three steps down of her own, Quinn forgot all about worries and let herself get caught up in wonder.

The sub-basement was much smaller than the room overhead, but just as carefully built. The walls and floor were remarkably straight-edged, almost as if they'd been laser-cut.

Once she got both feet on the floor and turned, she saw what Doug meant about the stairs. They were literally cut out of the bedrock, with no space underneath at all. She had no trouble imagining why a family coming from New England and England before that would have felt safe from fierce Midwestern storms down here.

The soft, mellow light came from several clear glass bulbs, bigger than she was used to seeing and strung in an X along the stone ceiling. She wondered for an instant whether the thick, black fabric-covered cord running between them would pass a modern inspection.

Then all of her attention was captured by a rough, sturdy wooden table and chairs in the middle of a space only about six of her steps across. Each were built of heavy pieces, with the table's legs easily a few inches thick. Not painted that she could tell, but naturally aged to a rich, dark shade. The square top wasn't much longer than her arm in either direction.

In the center of the table sat a gleaming wooden box, far too fine and delicate to be hidden away underground.

About five inches high, twice that deep, and at least a foot long, the top of the box was anchored by copper straps and hinges that shone bright as if they'd been polished the night before. A simple matching hinge that held the box closed without any way to lock it provided the only other decoration.

With streaks and stripes and swirls of different colors that seemed part of the wood, it really didn't need any other embellishment.

Doug stood beside the table, hands on his hips, grinning like a schoolboy.

"What kind of a treasure box did my grandmother leave for us?"

Quinn laughed, more caught up in his enthusiasm than she wanted to admit. And in the idea that his sweet, strong, no-nonsense grandmother would have left *anything* that involved Quinn herself.

"Have you ever seen it before?" She stood on the opposite side of the table and leaned down, hands on her knees. "It's beautiful. Looks like it was made of all different kinds of wood, but I can't see the joins."

He started to bend over himself, then picked up the chair in front of him and pulled it back. Quinn couldn't help a smirk at how he tried to shake the chair to test how solid it was before he sat. Strong as he was, he'd strained a bit to lift it.

She suspected the two of them could dance on that chair and it wouldn't shift an inch.

"Never seen it or anything like it," he said, sitting and lowering his face until it was almost on top of the box. "Or heard any mention of a mysterious special box, any more than the secret room we're in right now."

Quinn reached out and stroked the box with one finger.

"Not a spot of dust on it, and no one's been in this house for months. Who knows how long since anyone's been down here. How is that possible?"

Doug ran his fingers along the tabletop, making twin streaks that were much darker without their coat of gray.

"I'd like to learn that trick for myself. Want to do the honors?"

Quinn sat back, slowly shaking her head. She drew her hand back and folded both of hers on the dusty table.

"Not even one little bit. This is far outside my job description as your realtor." She smiled, not wanting to sound as harsh as all that. "Or even as your friend. You're up for this one, as today's designated Linton grandchild."

He reached across and covered her hands with his for a second, gazing into her eyes in a way that was somehow more intimate than the touch. Just before Quinn's heartbeat and breathing sped up too much to hide, he moved away, hesitated, and flipped open the latch.

Then grunted when he lifted the lid.

Inside were…ordinary envelopes.

No, not quite ordinary, not like bills and notices and such. These were made of thick, weighty paper, and the addresses were in metallic script.

More like expensive party invitations than anything else.

"What in the world…" Doug pulled one off the top and handed the next one to Quinn without looking at it.

She ignored a twinge suggesting she'd be better off not looking at anything his grandmother and possibly his great-grandmother and great-great-grandfather and beyond kept this well-hidden.

The envelope was addressed to Mrs. Cora Louise Linton in sparkling silver script, with delivery to the house they sat in. No sign of a postmark or stamp, or any scuffing or other sign it had spent time in a mail delivery bag.

Quinn's breath caught when she looked at the return address, smaller but in the same silver.

It at least appeared to be from a Ms. Quinn H. Linton, with a street address in Decatur, Georgia.

The same place Doug lived right now.

Someone had gone through a hell of a lot of trouble to try to pull some kind of sick, twisted joke.

She looked up without making any attempt to hide her distress and confusion—or the way her heart and stomach dropped like lead weights—right into green eyes showing the same thing.

"I don't understand this." He dropped his envelope with a copper-script address onto the table as if the feel of it disgusted him. "Did you... Did you send the attorney out here before you? Or someone else?"

"What? No, I didn't have time to send anyone out here, or reason to. I got the call a couple of days ago, just like I told you. Did *you* send someone else out here, Doug? Or get here early?"

He squeezed his eyes closed for a second and put his hands flat on the table.

"You saw me drive up, Quinn. That was when I got here. As far as I know, and going by what you say, no one else has been out here for weeks."

"Then what is this supposed to mean?" She put one finger on the corner of her envelope and pushed it toward him, letting it spin so he could read it. "I have to say this feels like some kind of bad middle school prank."

He scowled, then rubbed his forehead and ran his fingers through his hair.

"What kind of prank is this one, then?" He flicked the envelope in front of him toward her with his fingertips.

Same address embossed big and fancy in copper, to the Linton household. But the return was from Quinn Hedges and Doug Linton, with her exact street address in St. Louis.

Quinn was more furious than embarrassed, but she knew the flush creeping up her neck and face could look like either one to someone who didn't know her well.

Despite the last hour, she felt like she sat across from someone she'd never met in her life.

And someone she wasn't quite sure she should trust.

"This doesn't… What the hell is going on here?"

Doug threw up both hands and shook his head

"Good damn question." He flipped the St. Louis envelope over and tore it open, without a trace of concern for avoiding ragged edges.

Quinn opened hers more carefully, doing a neater job purely out of growing anger with spite floating around the edges.

"Really, Doug? This is supposed to be *funny* or something?" She all but threw the heavy embossed card at him. "An invitation to our tenth anniversary party, no gifts, but please RSVP?"

He raised his voice, making her wish she'd done the same.

"Yeah, I'm laughing my ass off over here. This one is for our twentieth, thank you very much. With a handwritten note to *my* grandmother letting her know *our* guest room in Atlanta is hers for the weekend!"

Quinn pushed her chair back, making a satisfying scraping noise across the smooth rock floor. She walked in a tight circle, wishing she had any whisper of a chance of keeping angry shaking out of her hands and voice.

Clenching her fists couldn't possibly make things better, but she couldn't stop herself.

"Fine then." She moved to stand close enough beside him that he had to look up at her. "What else is there in your magic box? Wedding invitations? *Birth* announcements?"

He moved his chair back more carefully, staring

into her eyes the whole time, his face as cold as she'd ever seen it.

"I hope I misunderstand you right now. You're not standing there accusing me of setting this up as some kind of awful joke, right? Especially because you're the only one who could have *possibly* done this. Even though I can't for the life of me imagine why."

"Me neither, Doug. Because believe me, I'm not finding any of this even a tiny bit funny."

He pressed his lips into a tight, pale line, then stood in one abrupt motion. Instead of moving toward the stairs or toward her, he took three deliberate steps toward the opposite wall and turned to face her.

"Go ahead, see for yourself. Or maybe I should say *retrieve* for yourself. Open as many as you want. Open them all. Tell me what the point of it all is, besides some bullshit story about a woman who's dead now and can't defend herself. A woman who loved you as much as—"

He took a slow, deep breath and crossed his arms.

"You should probably go," he said in a ragged voice. "Take whatever you want and go."

Quinn drew breath to argue, to protest her innocence, or maybe to yell at him for even suspecting such an absurd thing. Even if she had managed to get herself here early and somehow found the hidden room, she would have never done such a bizarre and cold-hearted thing.

Pretending to create...whatever this was, and making it look like his grandmother was behind it all. Quite successfully using their shared past as a vicious wedge.

But someone had.

And she had no idea whether they'd been targeting her or Doug, or why.

Or whether Doug himself was behind the whole thing, and his upset right now was nothing more than another game.

"The only thing I *want* is to understand who thought this was worth doing. Who thought going to all this trouble would accomplish anything." She tipped the box up, spilling the pile of envelopes across the table. "Want to fess up before I walk out of here?"

Doug closed his eyes for a second and tilted his head to the side. When he opened them, they were rimmed with red.

"I didn't do this, Quinn. I wouldn't. You have to know me better than that."

Quinn let out a bitter laugh that threatened to bring up all the rich cake and coffee right behind it. Unwilling to leave all of the evidence behind, she scooped up half the envelopes.

"Yeah, well. I thought you knew *me* better than to even think something like this of me. Looks like we're both the fools today, huh?"

She turned and walked up the steps, forcing herself to go slowly. The thought of tripping and either making an ass of herself or tumbling down sharp-edged stone was all that kept her from doing her best to run.

Whatever it took, she had to get away.

Chapter 14

Doug stared at the bedrock under his feet, refusing to watch Quinn walk away, even though he'd told her to go. He didn't move or breathe until he heard a distant thud that had to be the kitchen door closing.

Then he slowly folded forward, catching his hands against his knees to keep from ending up on the cold stone floor.

What the hell just happened?

Whether he wanted it or not, shaking started up in his middle and spread into his arms and legs.

Distress caused part of it. The cause didn't make much difference when it came to her, especially after so many years apart.

Part of Doug was gutted to know she was walking, then driving out of his life again. Quite likely for the last time.

But more than enough of his trembling came from anger.

Was it possible she'd set this up? Planted the awful attempt at a joke, or some kind of coercion, or whatever the hell else she might have had in her mind?

He stood, leaning against the cool, rough wall and pressing his palms against it. A few deep breaths made it clear how much he was sweating despite standing more than twenty feet underground. Sweat that reeked with an acrid bite.

Try as he might, he couldn't manage to put Jenny or any of the rest of his family behind this…stunt. At a very basic level, they likely wouldn't have known where Quinn lived. And he simply couldn't imagine any of them wanting to do something like this.

Sneaking down here and planting this elaborate setting complete with props, and all for what? To point out that he and Quinn never had that history together? Or worse as far as he was concerned, trying to imply that his grandmother always wished it was actually true?

The horrible sadness he felt like he was drowning in the day she died threatened to surge up and choke him again. Too many painful questions and accusations, every one inside his own mind.

He'd been selfish to leave home when he did, abandoning both of his grandparents.

But why didn't he come back when his grandfather died? He should have helped care for her.

Then he knew she wanted him to handle the house when she did pass, and still, he stayed away.

Leaving that to Jenny, who had a hell of a lot more of a life keeping her occupied than he ever had.

There were engineering firms in St. Louis, too. It wasn't like he had a wife and kids to uproot. How hard would it really have been to bring a dog and a cat with him?

All of that made sense at the time because when he left, he *was* running away. From himself and his lack of focus. From the fact that however much he loved Quinn and (he thought) she loved him, they never could make it work for long.

Fear of returning back here and sinking into all the same destructive patterns didn't seem the least bit farfetched with the way his heart twisted and compacted in his chest.

But still, could she really have done *this*?

Doug walked to the table and moved the envelopes scattered across the surface until he could see more of the return addresses. The ones with some variation of his name and Quinn's only stirred up the anger, pushing aside the only question he really should be asking himself.

Why?

What could she possibly have hoped to gain by this?

And if she was telling the truth and she hadn't done this, who?

And again, why?

All of that lost its unsavory forward momentum when he spotted a different name. Supposedly from his house in Georgia, same as many of the others.

But sent from Mare and Doug Linton instead.

Chills raced over his flesh, and not only because the cold of the sub-basement seemed to be sinking into his bones.

He couldn't recall ever mentioning Mare to his grandmother, and he hadn't said her name out loud to Quinn. And close as he and Mare had been and still were, their romance burned far too hot and fast to even consider marriage.

Another shuffle showed one that had him sinking down to the uncomfortable chair.

From an address in Washington state, where he'd never set foot in his life or even contemplated living. With himself and Sherrie Weston, a woman he'd dated for a few years at his first engineering firm. She'd at least come with him on a visit to Illinois toward the end of their uncomfortable match.

But she was from New Hampshire, not Washington.

The last had him covering his mouth with a newly trembling hand.

Alexandra Stevens, written as Alex S. Linton. Supposedly mailed from Destin, Florida. Doug had actually been to Destin, on vacation with Alex while they were together during his drifting days in Atlanta.

And again a couple of years later, but that trip was nowhere close to a vacation.

He'd gone for Alex's funeral.

Shaking his head, Doug got to his feet as he pushed all the envelopes back into the wooden box. He flipped the latch closed, then carefully put the chairs back as they were when he walked down here.

He hesitated for a second, fingertips on the box's lid. It really was as smooth as glass, without a trace of where the different bits of wood were joined.

Taking it out of here didn't feel like a mistake, not exactly. All the damn envelopes had his name on them in some form or another, after all. So it only followed that he had every right to see what was inside each of them if he wanted to.

If he could stand to.

He wondered for a second if Quinn would be able to stand looking at the ones she'd taken.

Either way, sitting deep under his grandparents' house for even one more minute felt like a slow-moving nightmare that would only gain force and momentum if he didn't get himself out of here.

He curled the box under his arm, making sure the opening faced up. He doubted he'd have the mental or emotional strength to gather the blasted things up again if they spilled.

Everything together only weighed a few pounds, but he somehow felt like he carried a hundred or more up the stone steps as he went.

Doug looked back at the table from the top, wondering anew at how the box hadn't shown a trace of dust. He could see new streaks and smudges in the table's thick coat even in the dim light.

From this angle, he spotted another of the old fashioned two-button switches in front of the typical flip version that controlled the lights. In this case, only one was pushed in.

He flipped the lights off on the way back into the basement, and the old incandescent lights gave a distinctive tink as they faded to black.

He leaned back down and pushed the other button down, and sure enough, the grinding noise under the furnace started up again.

An odd lack of dust was by nowhere near the strangest thing he needed to deal with. Doug watched the concrete complete its slow path back toward the wall, then turned to go.

A gust of cold, rainy wind hit him as soon as he stepped outside, intensifying the impression that he must have imagined sitting out here with Quinn. With the way he felt right now, the idea of their friendly, even flirty conversation felt worse than a fairy tale.

But not as bad as her kiss.

Unless he wanted to chicken out and run back to Georgia and leave Jenny overwhelmed and dumped on, Doug was going to have to at least communicate with Quinn at some point.

But not right now.

Right now he had to deal with a sneaky little doubt he had no intention of ignoring until it got a secure foothold in his mind.

By the time Jenny picked up on the third ring, he was already turning onto the bigger gravel road with the call routed through the Jeep's stereo.

"Hey Doug! Too busy out on the farm to give your cousin a call and let me know how it's going, huh?"

Doug laughed with her, relieved he didn't have to make it look realistic. Trying to make it sound that way was hard enough.

"Something like that. I am sorry to bother you, I know you're running ragged. How's everyone doing?"

He heard a door closing and a long sigh.

"Well, you know. Not much more than a few naps here and there, but they're all healthy and happy. So that means everyone is wonderful. I think this is the first time Mom, Dad, and Baby Ian have been asleep at the same time, so Granny and Papaw are catching our breath. What's happening there?"

"I'm glad they're all settling in. The house looks pretty good, but things are kind of strange. Have you heard from the attorney since…you know, since all this stuff about the will came up?"

Instead of spitting rain he could ignore, a sudden noisy downpour hit the Jeep, almost as if he'd driven into a vast, invisible carwash. Doug flipped on the wipers and the headlights, hoping the instant sludge he couldn't quite see through cleared before he got to roads with traffic.

The thought of a new baby brought Quinn asking if there were birth announcements in the box too sharply into his mind. Announcements of a child of theirs that had never happened in this lifetime, and never would.

"I haven't heard a word since she set up the walk-through," Jenny said. "Which I don't think I've told you enough how much I appreciate you taking care of. What do you think of the realtor? Someone we can work with?"

Doug laughed under his breath, once again glad Jenny couldn't see his face.

"So you don't know who it is? Honestly?"

"Only a name, and I'm too sleep-deprived to remember what it was. Something strange, with a…a Q, maybe? That can't be right."

"It's right," he said, not sure whether he should be relieved Jenny and Quinn had never crossed paths or not. "Quinn Hedges."

"That's it, yeah. I guess that's who was specified in the will as the realtor, but I don't know why. Honestly, I didn't read any of it over before we found out Ian's arrival was imminent. Listen, if you have even a hint of a bad feeling about it, just say the word. I'm not so busy I can't ask around and find someone else."

Now Doug wished he could see Jenny's face besides in his imagination. Curly hair a brighter red than his, probably twisted into a bun that looked great even though she was tired. Likely an old blue and orange University of Illinois sweatshirt and leggings, unless she'd experienced an unlikely entry into fashion awareness with new grandmotherhood.

The truth was not seeing her didn't make any difference at all. He was more certain than ever that she wasn't lying to him. And that she'd had nothing to do with the damn box now riding in the cargo area of his Jeep with an old blanket tossed over it.

Right beside the cute little takeout box with food he couldn't throw out but couldn't imagine eating.

"I think the realtor will be fine as far as the house is concerned. The rest I guess will have to work itself out. What I really wanted to ask you about was the sub-basement."

In the silence, Doug turned the sound up to make sure he didn't miss her reply in the pounding rain inches above his head.

"I'm sorry, Doug, it must be noisy there. Did you say *sub*-basement? You don't mean at Grandma's house? There's only the basement there, right?"

"It's pouring rain here, but I did say sub-basement. I never heard about it either, but it's there, right under the furnace."

"*Wow*," Jenny said, her voice low and wondering. "What, did this Quinn person find it? What was down there?"

Doug opened his mouth, then snapped it closed hard enough that his teeth clacked painfully. Hard certainty crawled from his shoulders to his neck and into his brain.

Whether it made sense or not, he was certain telling Jenny about the box wasn't a good idea. His grandmother's letter made it clear it was for him.

"A wooden table and chairs. I guess it was a storm shelter when the house was new. Pretty bizarre cloak and dagger stuff for out in Middle of Nowhere, Illinois, huh?"

"I'll say. Hey, maybe that will bring us a higher sale price."

"It might. How are you feeling about that? Selling the house, I mean. We never did really talk about it before you told me about Ian's big arrival and I jumped in my four-wheel-drive chariot and headed north."

Doug stopped at the intersection with the first paved road, nothing more than a two lane that barely rated lines down the middle. He only saw a couple of sets of headlights in the distance, with plenty of room even in the rain that had settled in for a long stay.

But he waited anyway.

"We didn't, did we?" Jenny said. "I shouldn't have dumped all of this on you without even reading the damn will. I just assumed we were going to sell and split it with everyone, you know? The attorney said it was totally up to you and me, though. We don't have to clear it with anyone else, sell or keep. Are you wanting to move up here?"

Doug closed his eyes and shook his head.

Even if that thought had crossed his mind as lightly as a cloud passing over the moon, the best possible reason for such a big change had proceeded him down this same road. Probably at much higher speeds.

"I don't think so, no. I just wanted to check in with you."

"You don't believe you're going to sneak back down to Georgia without coming by here, do you? If so, I have an airtight pail full of dirty diapers to sneak into your car."

At least this time his laugh sounded real, and it almost felt real, too.

"Of course I'll stop by, especially when you put it that way. You still need to send me a picture of Ian, though. And show him one of me so the new cousinlet recognizes the bad influences in the family."

"Your first cousin, twice removed, though I doubt you'll remember that for five minutes after we're off the phone. I will do my best to remember to send you a whole phone-load of pictures. You okay, Doug? You sound kinda down."

Doug pulled out onto the paved road, heading toward his lakeside cottage and what promised to indeed be a kinda-down afternoon and evening.

"I'm okay. It's just tough seeing the house after so long. That's all. You're the one dealing with major life changes there, don't worry about me."

Jenny let out a hearty snort.

"Between you and me, I'm enjoying myself immensely. I get to be Mom-the-Hero for a few days, which is wonderful. I'll be happy to go back home to my infant-free house, too. I've got my phone on mute so I might have to call back, but you call me if you need to, understood? I did spring all of this on you. I know it's not easy."

"Understood. Thanks Jenny. I'll let you get back to it."

Doug ended the call and muted his own phone without even considering music.

He couldn't think of one song that would make him feel better instead of worse.

Not until he got himself together and figured out what was really going on.

Chapter 15

QUINN RELUCTANTLY EASED off the gas pedal when a horrendous downpour cut her visibility to near-zero.

She was off the graveled back roads, thank goodness. But she might have kept better traction there than on asphalt that gathered puddles slick with oil and road-gunk.

One thing the rain did was intensify the feeling that her car was a cockpit: the high-tech command center of a sleek machine that responded to her every wish.

Console and stereo lights set to warm blue, a curving dashboard and driver's area that fit her like a fine leather glove. A seat more comfortable and adjustable than anything in her house or anyone else's.

And that stereo was a beast when she was in the mood for it. Or, in a different mood, the car's excellent soundproofing let her hear the smallest note and detail of quieter music.

The fact that she could hear the rain so clearly let her know how hard it really was coming down.

Not quite as hard as her mood had come down back in that basement with Doug.

Her face, mind, and gut cycled between hot embarrassment and cold anger at the whole situation. One she couldn't simply avoid and pretend never happened since she'd agreed to handle the damn house.

The thought of walking back in there, though, especially with Doug, pushed her internal disruption close to active nausea.

She shook her head once, hard, in an old habit that sometimes worked to stop thoughts that were not welcome. Not quite hard enough to be an actual brain reset. But enough to get her gray matter's attention.

Not this time.

The corner of the car's map display screen blinked to let her know her next turn was coming up, and she'd at least be on a road with two lanes on each side.

Closer to St. Louis and home and her normal life with each mile.

Further away from whatever the hell was going on with Doug and that box full of envelopes.

For at least the twentieth time, Quinn considered grabbing the pile of them from the back floorboard and throwing them out the window. Odds were high they'd disintegrate before the storm ended, and that would be the end of the whole distressing mess.

Except it wouldn't.

She'd still know about the ones she'd seen and

read. And she'd be left wondering what was in the others.

That and what the whole stupid trick had been about in the first place.

She carefully accelerated onto the onramp, aware that even high-performance tires and her low-profile car wouldn't be a match for a sharp curve more like glass than pavement.

What a perfect way to top off a rotten day that would be.

Quinn wasn't sure what her next course of action should be, besides getting to her comfort friends and hopefully comfort food as fast as she safely could.

Call the attorney who'd given her this job? See if anything else suspicious had come up?

Or maybe, possibly, perhaps try to get Doug's cousin's phone number. That could be spun as innocent enough, since Jenny was the co-executor, right?

Sure, that made sense, *if* Jenny even knew what Doug was planning with that damn box. If not, then Quinn risked sounding more crazy than she already felt over the whole mess, and word of her call getting right back to him.

She drew in a deep breath, catching a trace of her early morning coffee and wishing she had more.

She'd never known Doug to be particularly good at hiding or faking his feelings. Or even a little bit interested in doing that, honestly. He was a lot more likely to let people know how he truly felt when he shouldn't.

Quinn had never seen him as upset as he'd been in that sub-basement, backing himself up into a corner like a terrified animal.

If she could somehow manage to step back from

her intense response for more than a few seconds at a time, she might even say he'd been more distressed than she had.

And that made no sense at all, not if he'd set up the awful hoax or joke or guilt trip or whatever it was meant to be.

She jumped and swore when her phone buzzed in her pocket and the car's display blinked again.

She was not ready to talk to Doug.

Not now.

Maybe not ever.

But because this day was clearly going to continue on following the same rotten theme, the call was from the only person she wanted to speak to *less* than Doug.

Jeff.

Getting in touch after days of his typical silence, with his normal dreadful sense of timing.

Quinn rolled her eyes and shifted her shoulders and back against the heated seat.

What the hell, maybe this would be a perfect way to distract herself. At least with Jeff, she felt a more or less friendly detachment. That had to be an improvement over the toxic slurry of anger, disgust, and heartbreak stirred up by the thought of Doug.

She stabbed at the little glowing green phone icon before she could change her mind.

"Hey Quinn! How's my favorite real estate tycoon doing?"

"I'm okay, Jeff. More like driving through a typhoon right now. What are you into today?"

"Looks like I'm into being stuck inside for the rest of the day. Just got back from Seattle, so I probably brought the rain with me. What got you out on a day like this, beautiful?"

Quinn raised one eyebrow and let a faint smile shift her stiff facial muscles. Jeff's exuberant way of speaking—and his constant travel for work—had seemed charming at first. Exciting, really.

Here was a guy who was into her and not afraid to say so, at least on a casual basis. *And* a guy who would be extremely unlikely to demand too much of her time or space since he was so seldom home.

Perfect match for someone who'd gotten tired of the whole dating/relationship thing a few years ago.

"I had a client out in Illinois," she said, "doing a favor for an old…family friend. Good trip?"

"*Great* trip. I think I talked our new hiking line up enough that I'll have more clients than I need by the end of the year. Missed you too much, though. What are you doing tonight?"

Quinn followed an offramp miles sooner than she needed to, ignoring her GPS's insistence that she should make a u-turn as soon as possible.

She was starving after her sugar binge earlier.

And despite her normal urge to drive as fast as legally permissible when she was upset, right now she wanted to sit still.

She also had no desire to serve her usual purpose of rescuing Jeff (and often herself) from boredom. All at once, she doubted she ever would again.

She didn't try to pretend she didn't have fun on their dates and nights together, not by a long shot. She usually had a *great* time that didn't mean much of anything to either one of them.

A nice arrangement when it worked.

For her at least, the whole thing had somehow turned sour.

Or maybe she'd finally admitted that to herself after way too long.

"I'm busy tonight, Jeff, sorry. Got some things to take care of. I'm sure you understand."

He paused, leaving her free to concentrate on navigating heavier traffic than she expected off the exit. Seemed like everyone decided the crowded shopping area would be the best place to hang out during a thunderstorm.

"Yeah, I understand, babe. Don't much like it, but I'm kind of surprised it took you this long."

Quinn parked beside one of a local chain of upscale Mexican restaurants that she'd loved since her high school days, glad to be off the road and able to concentrate on what Jeff just said.

He sounded more sad, maybe wistful, than angry.

Had her own voice been more harsh than she meant?

"I'm not sure I understand," she said. "You're surprised *what* took me this long?"

His laugh was good-natured, but again that melancholy tone.

"It's okay. No worries, right? We get along, have fun together, but neither one of us are really moving toward something longer-term. I knew you'd find something, or probably someone, who caught your interest more than me."

"Jeff, I don't... That's not what I'm trying to say."

"Eh, maybe not. But it's what's coming across, and I don't blame you one bit. I felt it in the air for a while now. We had some good times, Quinn. Not a thing in the world wrong with that."

Quinn leaned back against the headrest, rubbing her temples. Wishing she felt like making an argument or trying to convince him otherwise.

Wishing the *someone else* she'd indeed been considering hadn't turned into such a confusing, rotten headache.

"No, nothing wrong with that at all," she said. "I really wasn't trying to say that, but I won't lie. I have been thinking it lately. I'm sorry."

"I'm not sorry, not about getting to know you. If I ever do somehow become the settling down and stay in one place kind, I hope I can find someone a hell of a lot like you. Whoever's got your attention is damn lucky, and that's the truth."

Quinn tried to laugh and ended up choking back what felt way too much like a sob.

She'd somehow gotten herself into a state of mind where Jeff being so reasonable and decent to her made her feel worse than before.

"I don't know about that, but thank you for saying so. If you ever do get that urge to settle down, I'll only say congratulations and best wishes to you both."

This time his laugh bubbled up as uninhibited and joyful as usual.

"I wouldn't bet on that, but you never know, right? You okay?"

"I think so. I think I will be." Quinn wiped away a couple of tears, glad they weren't face to face after all. "Are you?"

"You know me. I'll be mopey for a day or so, then I'll be good as new. Take care of yourself, and make sure they treat you right. You deserve it."

And Jeff was gone.

Just a little bit before she was ready for him to be.

Quinn held her face in her hands for a few seconds, but she couldn't help smiling. It wasn't so much that she'd be sad, or miss him all that much. This wasn't a great upheaval for either of them.

She simply wasn't prepared, certainly not on top of the much bigger shock of the day.

Thank goodness the parking lot wasn't all that full. Besides wanting excellent food, she needed time and space to herself more than when she'd parked her car.

At the last minute, she grabbed the pile of envelopes and took them with her.

The decor was all muted orange and red and yellow inside the sprawling restaurant, with huge round tables in the sunken middle dining area, and bunches of private, secluded alcoves around the edges.

Several plants and trees thrived under broad skylights, in huge ceramic planters that coordinated with the brown tiles underfoot.

Quinn's stomach growled at the rich, spicy aromas of onions, peppers, and garlic as waiters delivered sizzling platters to a table near the lobby.

Within five minutes, she was tucked into a small booth close to the kitchen with no one else seated close by. Another few minutes brought a basket of fresh tortilla chips and salsa she was guaranteed to eat too much of.

Exactly what she needed, even though she declined one of their amazing margaritas with a rain-soaked drive still ahead of her.

Quinn stared out at the few crowded tables, at

people happy and laughing, or couples smiling and talking in lower voices.

Of course she and Doug had eaten at one of these, more than once. She'd be hard-pressed to find many restaurants around this part of Illinois that they'd missed.

As soon she gave the waiter her order for a much lighter meal than she actually wanted, she retrieved the envelopes from the chair beside her. She dropped the bunch of them onto the blue and yellow and white tiles on the table, running her fingertips across the heavy paper.

None of these had come off a department store shelf, and no home laser printer made that deep embossed script, either.

It wouldn't be hard to order things like this online now. No one was tied to the thick catalogs full of custom stationery she remembered flipping through for graduations and such when she was much younger.

She'd done the same for a wedding of her own a few years out of college. Quinn had been unwilling to make a big event of it, no matter how much pressure her family applied, or how badly Jeri and Bev wanted to handle the catering.

No big ceremony or reception, no fancy dress that cost a fortune. She'd even refused an expensive engagement ring—insisting on a perfectly nice cluster of garnets instead.

The one expense she'd allowed and taken care of herself was the fine, high-end announcements for after the fact.

She'd held onto them even after spending the money, with a sickening certainly she hadn't yet learned to trust in her twenties. When the marriage fell apart less than six months in, she'd burned them in a bonfire.

She pushed the pile over to the side when the waiter brought her guacamole, and took time to eat several scoops of chunky, perfectly spicy avocado goodness.

Then she arranged the envelopes into a neat stack so they all faced the same direction. About thirty of the cream-colored ones, every one still sealed.

But one plain white version stood out from the rest, longer and narrower like a bill or letter instead of an invitation. The kind you could buy in a box anywhere, even the grocery store.

Quinn's eyes blurred at the now-familiar handwriting on that one, so different from the expensive metallic printing.

For My Sweet Grandson.

She put that one aside. No matter how angry at Doug she was in the moment, opening a message in his grandmother's hand felt like a violation.

After a long drink of her Coke, with bubbles tickling her nose and the bittersweetness cutting the tightness in her throat, she twisted the stack so she could see the return addresses.

And her belly knotted up cold as the ice in her glass.

Not all of them appeared to come from some variety of her and Doug, or only from him.

Several were from Quinn herself. *By* herself or along with someone else altogether.

From her and the unfortunate and brief husband wasn't that much of a surprise considering what else had happened that day.

But the one from her and Jeri sent a flutter of unease into the emotional storm inside her mind and heart. From Ms. Quinn and Ms. Jeri Fitzsimmons-Hedges, to be exact.

Shaking her head, Quinn used the knife from the table to open the envelope. She couldn't quite manage to be surprised at the impressionistic watercolor image of two brides on the invitation inside.

"I don't understand any of this," she whispered, putting the knife down when she noticed how badly her hands shook.

She didn't bother opening the one supposedly sent from herself and Jeff.

Enough of this.

Quinn held both hands out, fingers spread wide, staring at them until they held steady.

She smiled and nodded when the waiter brought her food, and she knew she'd get the burrito down. Whether she felt like eating or not, it was too good to waste, and she knew her body was hungry no matter what her staggered mind said about it.

She closed her eyes for a second until she felt calm. For whatever reason, making this particular decision pushed her fear and confusion down to a low rumble inside.

Quinn opened the envelope from Doug's grandmother.

Chapter 16

Doug again sat on the little back deck of his lakeside cabin, green towels covering the damp wood of the chair, blanket draped over his legs.

The storm had finally let up about the time he got there with his cold takeout lunch, which he'd picked up from a cheap fast food place for some absurd reason. Even way out here, there were far better choices.

He at least could have waited until he got to Carlyle, so the hamburger and fries wouldn't be quite so rubbery and congealed.

It somehow made sense at the time, but now the unsatisfying food sat like a lump in his stomach.

The aroma of several more people cooking out than the night before didn't help.

This late afternoon, the lake was busier than the much nicer day before. No sailboats with the wind blown out by the storm. Plenty of fishing boats, thank goodness sitting anchored rather than buzzing around looking for the best place to cast in.

The sky had turned a high, dark blue, almost like a deep winter sky rather than autumn really coming on. Most of the leaves were in wet, mushy piles on the grass rather than rattling in the trees.

All their color faded out and fallen.

Doug had a tidy pile of opened envelopes on the table beside him, each with the invitation or announcement tucked back inside. The box itself waited on the granite counter in the cozy little kitchen.

He didn't understand what was happening any better than he had back at his grandparents' house. But he'd at least disarmed the surprises, assuming he never saw Quinn or the ones she'd taken with her again.

He'd read invitations to multiple weddings of his that never happened, anniversary party invitations for non-existent marriages, holiday greeting cards, birthday cards, and a birth announcement that made his heart ache.

Of course that child who would never be was supposedly with Quinn.

Her being involved made less sense than ever now. And he had no idea what else could possibly be going on.

He pulled his legs up into the chair, sitting cross-legged like a little kid.

He had Quinn's phone number, along with every reason to believe she wouldn't answer his call.

Jenny would hear how upset he was the second he opened his mouth. And the idea of eating into her precious new grandmother time with Ian before he'd even been in the world for a week felt selfish in the extreme.

Mare was probably the least fanciful person he knew, and possibly the most likely to ask pointed questions he wasn't ready to deal with right now. She'd sounded plenty suspicious when he called earlier to check on Maya and Prince, like she was saving up for a tremendous outburst of questions on the next call.

But he wasn't sure who else he could talk to.

Doug had done such a wretched job of keeping up with people he'd grown up with that his local options were sadly limited.

He'd just about decided to take his chances with Mare when he heard someone calling his name. When no one besides the owners of his cozy little cabin should possibly know he was there.

"Yeah? I'm around back."

Before he could decide whether to get up and investigate or hope the mystery person went away, a familiar but impossible figure walked around the corner to his right.

"Quinn?"

She stopped and stared at him, and to his utter surprise, she laughed. Not a mocking or disgusted laugh either, but an honest guffaw that had him smiling when he didn't think he could.

She wiped at her eyes and took a step closer.

"I'm sorry, Doug. For showing up like this, for laughing. For earlier today most of all. But you just… You look like a little old man on the deck of a cruise ship or something. And the map of Illinois is the perfect touch."

Doug's brain was so gummed up at seeing her that he actually had to look down at himself to have any idea what she meant. He had to admit the lap blanket and towels weren't exactly the height of fash-ion. Or sex appeal.

"You don't like it? I was going for Southern chic on vacation in the freezing Midwest, but I may have to recalibrate. Not that I'm not glad to see you, but why are you here? How did you find me?"

She stepped up onto the deck, accepting the towel he extracted from behind his shoulders to wipe down the other chair. Before she sat, she put a stack of envelopes on the table beside his.

They were all the same shape and made of the same paper, except for one ordinary version standing out bright white.

"I'll answer the easy one first. I remembered where you said you were staying. Georgia license plates are kind of few and far between in general, and especially this time of year. I know I should have called, and I truly am sorry about that."

She rubbed her palms against her thighs, making a faint rasping noise against her blue jeans.

"I thought about it the whole way here. Even pulled your number up on the phone and on the car's system. But every time I started to dial, I couldn't think of what I could possibly say. When I spotted your Jeep, I finally admitted I had no idea but it was too late to turn back."

"Okay. No need to apologize for being here. But I need to apologize to you for earlier today too. I didn't know then and I don't know now what's going on, or who's behind this. I do know it wasn't you. I'm sorry."

Quinn shook her head and crossed her arms.

"You read all of yours?"

Doug nodded, afraid to interrupt her. If she was willing to talk, he very much wanted to listen.

"This will sound strange," she said, "but were some of them sent…supposedly sent…with someone besides me?"

He raised his eyebrows and let out a breath.

"They were. All people I dated at some point, but they still didn't make sense. One of them… Never mind. How did you know that? Did you find some like that?"

He wanted to look at the stack she'd brought, and he got the feeling she wanted him to. He still couldn't seem to force his hand to reach over and get them.

"I mostly had ones that apparently came from you and me. I didn't see any from you and someone else, but I'm not surprised you found some. What really got my attention was the ones that seemed to come from *me* and someone else."

She handed the stack to him, and Doug managed to break his paralysis enough to examine the return addresses. He vaguely noticed she kept the white envelope before the variations of Quinn and partner took over his mind.

"Are these all people you dated? Like mine were?"

"All of them. One I married for a very brief time. And one I broke up with this afternoon. Well, I guess he technically broke up with me, but it's hard to say since most people would say we weren't really dating anyway."

Doug rubbed his forehead and tried to brush back his increasingly wild humidity hair. Quinn been married, and his suspicions about her dating someone now were true. He'd struggle to take in one of those information bombs at a time.

Both delivered so close together would surely prove impossible.

Instead he flipped through the stack with no idea what he was looking for.

"I honestly don't know what to say." One of the name arrangements caught his eye, and his mouth jumped in without consulting him. "Is Jeri the one you married? I didn't know… I mean…"

Quinn leaned over and touched his forearm, her warm hand lighting up his chilly nerve endings.

"Jeri isn't the one I married, no. But we did date for a while after college. She and her wife have been my two best friends ever since. That's a wedding invitation inside the envelope, though."

Doug managed a small smile, gratified that he could still be surprised by Quinn and this whole situation. He'd thought his mind had already absorbed too many today.

"I had one sent from a state I've never been to," he said. "The woman I was supposed to live there with wasn't even from there. And one woman I did date, but she… She passed away a long time ago."

Quinn lowered her head, and when she looked up at him, her eyes were red.

"That must have been awful, Doug, to lose someone like that. I'm sorry."

He shuffled through the stack one more time, but he didn't want to see what was inside any of them. Looking through the ones he'd brought was bad enough.

"We're talking around the big question, aren't we?" he said. "It's obvious they're not accurate or we wouldn't be sitting here. But who did this in the first place? And why?"

Quinn handed him the last envelope—the ordinary one—with a bittersweet smile. His heart thudded to a stop in his chest when he recognized his grandmother's handwriting for the second time that day.

For My Sweet Grandson.

"Was this with the others?" he whispered.

She nodded. "This is the next thing I need to apologize for. I think it must have been at the bottom, and I scooped it up with all the rest. I looked through the others when I stopped for lunch. I'd put that one aside because it wasn't meant for me. After I saw the rest, I had to know. I shouldn't have opened it. But you need to read it."

Doug very much wanted to hesitate, maybe even to tell her he'd look at the letter later. Tomorrow, even. Feeling equal measures of eagerness to read this message from beyond the grave and dread of what he might learn about his family only emphasized the greasy lump of bad food in his belly.

He slipped the folded paper out of the envelope instead. He was far more afraid of letting fear and inaction freeze him solid for the rest of his life.

He did pause long enough to blink his tear-blurred vision clear before he started reading.

My Dearest Doug,

First things first. Let me make this one thing clear, even if the rest may seem foggy to you for a while. The way this turned out—with you probably reading this after I've passed away from this life—is in no way your fault.

I had a thousand chances to share this with you, and I didn't.

You made the very good choice to move away and begin your own life, and you thrived because of that choice. Watching you discover your way to happiness has brought me great joy.

I could have spoken to you during the years before you left, even though you weren't ready. I could have done so on any of the many times you returned to visit me, even though I wasn't ready.

And so here we are.

This was my responsibility, my knowledge to pass on to you. I failed in this responsibility.

Any guilt must rest firmly on my side.

No arguments from you, now!

Doug stared out over the lake again as he turned the page, not bothering to wipe his tears now. He heard her voice, saw her flashing green eyes.

He knew very well how angry she would have been if he'd dared try that argument.

I don't know if I'll be able to venture down to my hide-away again after today. What your grandfather called my secret lair. When I close the box with this inside, it will be the only thing inside.

If any time passes at all before you see this, I'm quite sure it will be far from the only thing.

I do know this box has been in my family since long before we came to Illinois. I'm afraid I can only give you rumors for where it came from. Rumors probably more entertaining than informative. Yet entertaining enough that I wrote as many of them down as I could over the years. Along with many of the things I found in the box that never came to pass.

You'll find those notebooks with the other books I'll take with me if I move to another place, as so many people who care about me want me to. If I pass at home, which I'd prefer, they'll be with the books beside my bed.

All the things I retain enough optimism and hope to believe I'll finish before my time comes to an end.

As for the contents of the box you're likely staring at with a healthy dose of mistrust, I'll only say this. I've come to believe it functions as sort of a time capsule that works in ways known only to whoever built it.

Not the typical time capsule that might be stuffed full of what people guess might matter in fifty or a hundred or a thousand years, assuming anyone remembers where they left it.

Our time capsule seems to deal in possibilities. And I've seen many changes with the times, to forms acceptable to modern eyes.

You'll likely find announcements and notices of events that came true. I found out about my own wedding, yes, but to more than one man, and in more than one place. I read about children who I later held in my arms, and those who only existed in some other place I don't claim to understand. I hope they're happy there.

I also don't understand why the enchantment of the box chose me rather than my brother or sisters, any more than why it chooses only one member of our family in each generation. Until it came to my own children, when it skipped ahead.

I understand that it has chosen you, and did so before you were born.

I don't ever wish to influence your choices in life, Doug, or sour what you know in your heart you want and need.

But I'll tell you I found items that mentioned your grandfather long before I met him.

You'll know in your own heart who has shown up right

alongside you time after time. In this strange and wonderful time capsule, and in your life.

I wish I knew why we have this gift, and this burden. I hope you'll be thankful to be chosen, as I was. I know you'll be wise enough to decide what to do about it now and in your future.

I wish more than anything I could talk to you about it now.

I love you, Sweetheart.

Grandma

Doug turned to Quinn, who stared out across the lake.

"Did you read the whole thing?"

She nodded without looking at him.

"Did you?" she said.

"The whole thing. I don't…" He folded the letter and put it back into the envelope, then rubbed his face. "I don't have any idea what to say or do. Except to tell you I'm glad you're here. And I'm sorry."

She finally turned to him with her head tilted.

"Sorry?"

Doug waved one hand in the air, wishing he could find words that didn't feel like they were ripping through his brain.

"What she said, about this being a gift and burden? That's the thing that makes the most sense of all to me. What are we supposed to do now? See, there it is, I just assumed *you're* going to do any damn thing, saying *we*, when you didn't have any more choice in this than I do."

He stopped, shaking his head and watching one of the fishing boats getting underway. The good-sized blue and white craft was far enough away that the buzzing of the outboard motor didn't start until a few seconds after it started to move.

"We have *all* the choices, Doug. You and your grandmother both said it. What we're reading with most of these isn't accurate. They're only possibilities. The decisions we've made at every turn brought us here. Because we were free to decide."

Rather than grabbing the whole stack to throw into the lake, Doug crossed his arms.

"Then what's the point of it? Just to torment us with what might have been? The mistakes we've made? All the better choices we had and ignored every time?"

When he looked at Quinn, he wished he'd thrown everything after all, and added the box for good measure.

Her serene and only a little amused smile made it clear she'd already gotten a long way toward knowing what to do here, at least for herself.

While he was still trying to figure out where to start.

Chapter 17

QUINN LET HERSELF TAKE A GOOD, long look at Doug. The longest since watching him drive up staggered her so badly the day before, certainly.

Probably the longest of the last few times they'd tried and failed to stay together so many years ago.

She couldn't remember the last time she'd only observed rather than trying to push herself away from him by finding fault, or trying to judge every part of him through the prism of her upset or hurt feelings.

Or remind herself how many times she'd walked away from him with a broken heart so she'd have the courage to do it again.

The lines around his eyes and mouth were deeper now than that morning, probably because he was confused and upset. But she saw how many of them reflected smiles and laughter rather than anger.

The tension of trying to live up to everyone's expectations—including his own, demanding even when they were in high school—had fallen away from him over time. This wasn't a boy or a young man struggling to find his way, fighting his own tendencies and talents instead of learning how to live and grow within them.

This was a solidly grown man. One who'd honestly considered those roles and dreams and situations that were never going to fit him.

And rather than forcing himself to keep going in all those wrong directions, he'd turned away. Turning toward his own path that would suit and satisfy him in the end.

Much like all the events in the Linton family time capsule that didn't happen simply faded away, with nothing left but the reminders of choices left behind.

"Did you get a good look at the dates?" she said. "On all those announcements?"

He shrugged and shook his head, which wasn't exactly saying no.

More a way of saying *so what?*

"The thing I noticed is even though the envelopes look brand new," Quinn went on, "and like your grandmother said, they fit what we expect with our modern eyes, the dates are still in the past. All the ones I looked at matched up with that time in my life."

He moved his shoulders again, this time rolling and relaxing them.

"That's what I saw, too. Everything they announced was set in the right time instead of now. Still, I keep coming back to why. Why would this happen at all?"

Quinn shook her head.

"I don't know why. I can't even guess. Maybe there's more about that in what your grandmother wrote. In her notebooks. All those rumors and stories. I have to admit I wonder if she ever found warnings. Things that might have gone a different way, or even bad things that hadn't happened yet. I didn't see any from the future in mine."

"No, neither did I. But we don't...I mean *I* don't know the rules of the time capsule yet, you know? Maybe that will happen when the designated family member takes possession of it. Physically, mentally, some other way I can't guess yet. It might have been in limbo or something until she passed away."

Quinn held her breath for a few seconds, wondering if she could slow her heartbeat or still the warm, looping sensation in her belly and chest.

She was a fully grown-ass woman herself, with a lot of her own ill-fitting expectations and plans comfortably in her past. Not to mention a satisfying number of decisions and choices that turned out for the better. And more of those happening as she got older and learned how to pay attention, and how to say no.

But at the moment, she felt like an awkward, scared kid all over again.

"You changed from *we* to *I* just then," she said. "So let me ask you this. Why do you think there were so many things in the time capsule that included me? Even things that didn't mention you at all?"

She suspected he tried to stop it, but a smile flitted around his lips. He started to look away, then turned to face her.

"I did wonder about that. Same way I've always wondered why we kept getting pulled back together over the years, even when we tried to stay apart. Until I pretty much ran away to stop it from happening again." He let out a long, slow breath, then held out his hand. "You ever wonder if all those times we split up might have been the mistakes? And this might be our chance to finally make the *right* choice?"

Quinn only hesitated for a second, listening to all the warnings and cautions and voices of reason from her mind. Letting them float through, simply noticing them without reacting.

When she instead surrendered to the welcome relief from her heart— twining her warm fingers through Doug's cool ones—her whole body exploded into fireworks.

"The thought has crossed my mind," she said. "This might be the time to admit I also thought about trying to track you down a few times after you ran off. After you escaped. But I talked myself out of it." She squeezed his hand as she brought it to her lips for a quick kiss. "That was probably for the best for both of us, though. Maybe we needed time to grow up on our own before..."

She bit her lip, unnerved by what she'd been about to say. Not because the words weren't true.

More because saying them out loud felt like a course correction that might affect her entire life.

Doug returned the favor by holding his lips against the back of her hand long enough to send goosebumps down her arms and legs.

"Before... I'm not sure I want to risk guessing what you were going to say. In fact, I know I'm not taking that chance."

Quinn leaned her head back and stared at the intensely blue sky, more like a vast overhead dome someone had painted rather than anything in nature.

She let that incredible color keep her calm, while Doug's hand now warm in hers gave her courage.

"Maybe we needed time to work out who we were," she said. "Who we *are*. On our own terms, with only ourselves to worry about. We were so young when we first got together. We would have cut off all those years of experimenting and figuring it all out."

When she looked at Doug, the deeper lines on his face were gone. Like a distressed part of him had relaxed.

"That could be why I left the way I did, yeah. Took off to where I knew for damn sure nobody would know me, or anything about my life or who I was. I certainly learned how to make decisions, and mistakes, for nobody but me. You think we might have a chance of getting past all the mistakes we made together?"

"No way," she said, smiling to soften the words. "If we want to see what might happen, we have to leave all that stuff right where it is, no matter what the magic box says. Our history would have to stay in the past. We already know how to *not* make it together."

He returned her smile and leaned closer.

"So we'd be starting out as grownups and get to know each other all over again. We do have a hell of a lot of new stories to tell."

"Maybe a *few* of the old ones," Quinn said, shifting toward him. "Some of those are pretty good. Like that weekend we spent out here at the lake."

"I wondered if you remembered that. One of the best weekends of my life."

Echoes of all that pleasure, all the passion

between them, lit up Quinn's insides with a rippling flash like distant summertime lightning.

"I never forgot a single minute."

She closed the distance between them, letting all of her questions and fears and hesitation dissolve in his kiss.

Even though the chemistry and heat between them had never once been a problem, Quinn had no doubt the memory would pale beside their new reality.

If they had the courage to try.

Doug finally drew back, cheeks flushed and breathing harder. He didn't let go of her hand.

"You have no idea how much I don't want to mention this, but there's one big problem with having a few years of our lives behind us. More than one, really."

Quinn raised one eyebrow, still breathing harder herself. "You mean our lives? All the structure and arrangements and obligations? In two different parts of the country?"

He inclined his head toward her.

"That's exactly what I mean."

She reached up and slipped her fingers into his hair and pulled him into another kiss. This time he was the one trying to keep her from pulling away.

"We have a hell of a lot of stuff to deal with," she said. "You're right. And you didn't even mention the time capsule, which I'm sure will play some kind of role. I'm willing to see what happens."

Doug closed his eyes for a second, and a blissful smile broke across his dear face. He stood in one easy motion, throwing his blanket back onto the chair.

"I'm willing to find out with you. Come inside

with me? There's an actual bed rather than a couple of sleeping bags in a tent."

Quinn took his offered hand and let him pull her to her feet, then squeezed him tight into a long, hard kiss.

Oh yeah, things between them promised to be different in so many ways.

And she was sure this specific, spectacular thing was going to be even better.

"I'm sure we'll manage to suffer through the discomfort of a bed somehow."

Chapter 18

DOUG STEPPED out onto the deck, wearing sweatpants and socks, again wrapped in his Illinois blanket. He'd already resigned himself to stealing it and leaving enough cash to cover the replacement with the cottage's owners.

Despite the mind-blowing past several hours—with an entirely sensible break for dinner delivery—he gasped at the unbelievable number of stars overhead. After so many years spent mostly under the orange-tinged skies of Atlanta, he'd forgotten the view miles away from any kind of city lights.

Even with the moon already set and unable to brighten up his surroundings, he could still see the deck and yard and trees. The lake had transformed itself into a glittering black blanket.

The aroma of his distant neighbors grilling and the sound of boats on the water were gone. The fresh, clean scent of the water and grass after a huge storm and the faint ripples took their place.

He knew he should be exhausted after such a

tumultuous couple of days, not to mention the intense pleasure of getting to know Quinn's body again, and the overwhelming way his reacted to hers. The thought made nerve endings all over his skin and much deeper inside flare into life again.

But he knew just as well he needed to…adjust his restless mind.

Give himself a chance to settle into an altered reality.

Doug thanked all the gods of friendship that Mare was a confirmed night owl. Not the best fit for him when he was into his normal routines of getting up early for work, perhaps. But perfect for when he slipped into this kind of nighttime mental gymnastics.

She picked up on the first ring.

"You *finally* ready to tell me what you were so upset about earlier?"

Doug laughed at her Southern drawl—exaggerated for effect—doing his best to keep it quiet. Quinn hadn't moved a muscle when he eased himself out of bed and tucked the heavy blankets around her. He was sure she needed the sleep as much as he would when he finally settled back down.

"I suppose I owe you that much. Only if you tell me how the creatures are doing first."

"You know they're doing wonderfully, even with my nocturnal ways. Maya is pushed so hard against my side that I'm pretty sure I'll have a bruise in the morning. And Prince has deigned to drape his warm, purring self over my shoulders while I read."

"They're a sucker for you, Mare. That much never changed." He walked out to the edge of the deck, wishing he'd stopped long enough to put on shoes so he could walk through the damp grass. "I get the feeling everything else changed over the last few hours."

"Ohhhhh, *do* tell. Unless you've run into some other long-lost love of your life, I imagine Quinn is somewhere nearby right now?"

"That she is. We had quite an evening together."

"To the surprise of no one, except maybe the two of you. All good?"

Doug wasn't sure he could find the words, but he wanted to give it his best effort.

"All is amazing. I don't know what will happen at the end of the week, or even tomorrow, honestly. I can't wait to find out. There's too much to tell you until I get it settled in my mind. Some of it strange enough that I don't even know how to start. But yeah. Amazing."

"That's pure music to my ears, my friend. You deserve someone who makes your voice sound exactly that dreamy every single day."

"Well, maybe not every day," Doug said, but he couldn't stop what he was sure was a dopey grin. "But I hope more often than not. We'd have a lot of stuff to work through. Houses, jobs. Living over five hundred miles apart. Simple things like that."

Mare laughed, and Doug heard one of Maya's yawn and howl combinations in protest.

"That stuff is simple, Doug, and you know it. We live all of four *miles* apart, remember? That wasn't enough, and that's nothing either of us did wrong. We just didn't work for that kind of relationship. Every single thing you mentioned can be changed in some way. Or sold, or adjusted. Whatever it takes. The only thing I can think of that would call an immediate halt would be if Quinn despises dogs or cats, right?"

"I haven't seen her with a dog or cat, if that's what you're asking. She loved the photos of my beasties, though. That has to be a good place to start."

"It's a perfectly lovely place to start. I hate to change the subject, because you know love and sex are two of my *very* favorite subjects, but what are you thinking about the house now? The farmhouse, I mean?"

Doug turned and looked up at the bedroom window, still dark, hopefully with a still sound-asleep Quinn.

"That's a good point. I guess I actually have a house in both places, don't I? Or I'm an executor on the one here, anyway. That's so much more complicated now." He shook his head, not sure how on earth he could begin to explain the time capsule. "The house itself isn't that hard, not really. But we found something…really strange there. I don't know what to say or even think about that, not yet."

Mare breathed in and out, slow and deliberate enough to carry over all those miles and connections.

"Is this the kind of thing that could hurt either one of you? Physically hurt you? Or any other way that matters?"

"No, I don't see how. Not as long as we both keep a clear head about it. If we really do decide to go for it, we'll have to keep clear heads about everything, right?"

"You sure will," she said. "Then one more question. I think Maya would like me to take her out for a late-night ramble now that she's awake. You're more than welcome to join us for more of a chat, but I'm going to hazard a guess you should get back to your company."

A stray gust of chilly wind found its way under Doug's blanket just then, leaving him shivering. And a warm bed with Quinn in it sounded like paradise.

"I should get back inside, yes. Ask away."

"Is this strange thing something you can bring with you when you come back? Because of course you must come back and reunite with these gorgeous creatures no matter where you decide to live. Before you ask, yes I will insist on seeing anything that you sound so *spooked* by."

"Spooked is a gentle way to put it," Doug said. "Even though I'm feeling better than I was this morning by a long way. I suppose I could bring it with me. Quinn mentioned having two best friends of hers take a look tomorrow, which I'm fully aware is a chance for them to meet and evaluate me. I'll want you to do the same as soon as I can get her down to Atlanta or you up here. I'd love to get a second, and third, and however many outside opinions as we can gather up."

"Good, because I'm curious like you wouldn't believe, about Quinn and this strange thing you've found. Be sure and let me know how this trial by her best friends goes. What you and Quinn think of each other matters the most, but friends say an awful lot about a person. Which is one reason I definitely want to meet her as soon as possible so I can make my usual good impression."

"I know you'll like her. And you'll score me points as a prime example of a good friend, which can't hurt."

"I certainly will. Now you go back to your lady friend while I take *this* lady friend out to do her thing. I'm sure Prince would like privacy to do all his bizarre cat things. You sound a hell of a lot better to me than you have for a long time, Dougie. I have to say if that's because of Quinn, then you get to work and arrange whatever you have to arrange to make this happen."

Rather than his usual protest at a nickname he'd never much liked, Doug only smiled.

"I'll see what I can do. Thanks, Mare. Give the critters a hug and kiss from me, and have a good night."

After another long, skin-tingling look at the bright swath of stars overhead and their reflection in the lake, Doug headed back inside.

In search of the person who warmed his body and his heart like no one else ever had.

Chapter 19

Mrs. Cora Louise Linton would have been full of pride at how bright and cheery her kitchen looked—and more importantly—how amazing it smelled.

Quinn wasn't the only one who suspected simply having people in the kitchen, getting ready to eat together, and happy to be there made all the difference.

The sad, dingy feel had vanished under much less scrubbing and dusting than anyone expected. Nothing more than a quick sweep through and opening the sturdy double-hung windows to the crisp early afternoon air.

Now the cheery curtains fluttered their crop of daisies into the room with a promise of new life, even in autumn.

The big family-sized table was set with heavy burgundy plates with forest green cloth napkins, and the most adorable flatware with flowers all along the handles. Jeri and Bev exclaimed over how gorgeous the Lintons' everyday kitchenware was every time they turned around.

Most of all at how several of the amazing iridescent cut-glass vases, bowls, and platters waited, simply tucked into cabinets as if they were perfectly ordinary.

One of the vases that was nearing a hundred years old now held a fresh bouquet of yellow black-eyed Susans, pink and purple asters, and huge lacy orange fronds that looked like giant ferns. All courtesy of the same local farm that supplied Bev's bakery.

Quinn and Doug did their best to follow orders when Jeri and Bev arrived, carrying in an intimidating number of boxes and containers. All while Doug good-naturedly answered an endless stream of questions and Bev worked the ancient and unfamiliar powder blue stove as if she'd last used it the day before.

Like Quinn halfway suspected they would when she called, Jeri and Bev had gone way overboard in bringing enough Sunday brunch for at least eight.

Quinn also suspected the four of them would manage to put most of it away without much trouble at all.

She'd already gotten two mugs of heavenly coffee down herself, and impatiently awaited more. Her stomach wasn't even pretending to be patient with the smell of an herb-filled quiche, fresh orange juice for mimosas, and cinnamon rolls floating throughout the house.

She and Doug kept themselves busy moving more slowly through the downstairs rooms than they had during the walkthrough, brooms and dust rags in hand. Opening all the windows to let the fresh air and cross-breezes wash away the accumulated loneliness and neglect.

They'd arrived early to explore the huge garage/barn hybrid, all of the warren-like rooms packed full of equipment and tools and projects. Enough to keep an antiques hunter or museum curator busy for weeks.

Wandering through hand in hand, guessing at the purpose or even the historical era of what they saw, reminded Quinn of their visits to flea markets and festivals and craft shows all those years ago. Not exactly typical late teen or early twenties dating behavior.

Almost as if they'd started out as a long-term, comfortably married couple before either of them graduated from college.

All that history made this reconnection or reunion or whatever it was feel all the more satisfying.

Maybe as long as the two of them put aside what they'd started and abandoned, they'd be free to move forward together in a different way.

One thing that remained unchanged but shockingly new was the way their bodies fit together the day—and the night—before. Quinn watched Doug reaching up to knock down cobwebs around the top of a doorway, enjoying the view without the faintest trace of sneakiness or guilt.

His jeans and t-shirt outlined his body in a perfectly scandalous way. Handsome as he'd always been, the years passing had added a strength to his back and shoulders, a muscular definition to his legs and backside.

Much like those same years added a patience and

practice to his lovemaking that had her closing her eyes and smiling at the heat of memory.

"What's got you smiling like that?" he said, crossing the crowded living room to stand beside her. They'd agreed right away that dusting the impressive collection of books and knickknacks and photos could wait for another day as long as they dealt with the worst of the mess.

She wholeheartedly agreed with his choice to wait on the final decision on the house itself, too, after a quick call to his cousin that morning. One life-changing event at a time, thank you very much.

Quinn opened her eyes and reached for his hands, pulling him close and breathing in the newly familiar scent of his skin and hair.

"I'm afraid to say. You'll quite rightly accuse me of being sentimental and sappy."

"Then we'll be a matched set yet again." He kissed behind her ear, grazing his teeth along her skin and raising chills all over her body. "I was thinking about the time we went out behind the barn at sunset with my whole family here. First time I ever had sex with someone on top."

"Okay then," Quinn said, giggling despite her efforts not to. "I was thinking how great your ass looks in those jeans. You use it to great advantage in bed, too." She squeezed him back there for emphasis, getting a satisfying groan in return.

"You are more than welcome to test that out again tonight," he whispered against her ear. "Your place or my temporary cabin by the lake?"

"How about mine? I'm guessing you haven't spent any time in St. Louis in ages."

"You got it. And I'd love to." He kissed the tip of

her nose and stepped back. "I need to ask you a question, and I'm afraid it's going to come out stranger than I mean it to sound."

Quinn crossed her arms and leaned against the wall.

"Go ahead. I think I'm more or less prepared."

He smiled like a shy kid and ducked his head.

"This is the Jeri you were involved with, right?"

Quinn shrugged and nodded at the same time.

"One and the same. Does that bother you?"

"Not one bit. She's obviously very much in love with Bev. And both of them care a lot about you. I don't think I've ever been so well questioned outside of a doctor's office or job interview."

"Good," Quinn said. "Jeri and I work a lot better as friends than we ever did as lovers. Bev's her perfect match, anyway. You keep saying I need to visit Atlanta. Who can I expect to handle my thorough questioning on your behalf?"

He laughed. "A few people, but mostly my friend Mare. She's the one staying with Maya and Prince right now. Our attempt at dating turned out a whole lot like you and Jeri, really. We're much, much better as friends."

Quinn reached for his hands again, relieved to feel not a trace of jealousy about an old girlfriend sleeping in Doug's house. After all, *her* old girlfriend was in the kitchen right now, hopefully almost finished with the brunch her stomach was constantly growling for.

"Then I'll look forward to visiting so I can meet her," she said. "Even more so I can meet Maya and Prince. I'm more worried about *them* liking me than any human."

He started toward her with every appearance of planning to kiss her again when Jeri cleared her throat with dramatic flair from just outside the living room door.

"Is it safe to come in there?" she called. "We need to borrow Quinn for a second, and you still haven't shown us this bizarre thing we just *have* to see."

"They need to discuss me with you, right?" Doug said with a grin. "Make sure I pass the first round of tests before they agree to feed me?"

"Pretty much any test you can think up will be worth it for Bev's food," Quinn said. "She made that gooey butter cake, remember? The coast is clear, Jeri."

Jeri swept into the crowded living room, peeking between her long fingers before she laughed and waved both hands. Today she wore jeans and an old t-shirt like everyone else, but even with her wavy black hair pulled into a ponytail, her tall and rangy frame managed to look elegant.

"Quinn is not only failing miserably to keep her voice down today," she said, "she's also right about Bev's food. I doubt the test has yet been invented that could keep me away. Everything is just about finished, so go grab your great mystery so we can eat while it's still hot."

"On my way," Doug said with a half-bow. "I promise to take my time, and I sincerely hope I'm allowed back inside when you're finished."

He winked on his way out as Quinn and Jeri walked arm in arm toward the kitchen.

"I'll save you the trouble of asking," Jeri said. "Even though you don't need our approval for a damn thing. Doug seems like a real sweetheart. And he's a total goner for you."

Warmth moved through Quinn's hungry belly at the words. Despite Jeri's words, of course her and Bev's opinions mattered.

"He's always been a sweetheart," Quinn said. "At least to me. I honestly never fell out of love with him, not even after so many years. And I gotta say if last night is any indication, that spark between us grew up into a blast furnace."

"Well, if anyone deserves that kind of blast, and that kind of bliss, it's you." Jeri squeezed her arm. "This is entirely selfish of me, but I do hate the thought that you might leave us."

Quinn leaned her head on Jeri's shoulder. She wasn't ready to think about moving, or ready for that inevitable discussion with Doug.

"We're nowhere near that point," she said, "or even talking about it yet. I plan to go down there in a couple of weeks for sure, partly because it's only fair for his friends to cross-examine me. But I don't know what's going to happen."

They walked into the kitchen to see Bev sitting at the table sipping from a steaming mug, with three others freshly poured. Doug's grandmother would have beamed at how insanely good everything still tucked away in the oven smelled.

"Fair enough," Jeri said. "Anything to say, Bev, before Mr. Handsome and Wonderful comes cruising back in here?"

Bev smiled and winked at Quinn.

"Not a thing I can add with the way they're both wandering around in a love-struck haze. I've never seen you like this, Quinn, not one time. If you're both ready, I say grab on with both hands and never let go."

Quinn leaned down for a one-armed hug before she sat in front of her own cup of coffee.

"I'd never assume I know what the future might bring," she said. "Certainly not after the last few days. But holding on this time is what I'm going to try my level best to do."

They all turned when Doug opened the kitchen door, then covered his visible ear with one hand.

"Am I allowed back in yet?"

Bev rolled her eyes, but she was smiling.

"We're finished with our discussion, for now. You can stay for brunch. The evaluation will continue, but I get the feeling you already knew that."

He made a show of wiping his brow with the back of his hand on the way to the table. The laughter stilled when he put the wooden box in the middle of the table and sat beside Quinn.

"Ohhhh, it's a mystery *box*," Jeri said, leaning forward but keeping her hands on her coffee mug. "Where did it come from, and what does it do?"

Quinn locked gazes with Doug for several seconds before she smiled and nodded. They'd talked on the drive over about how much to tell to be honest, but not enough to upset anyone.

Including themselves.

Doug did take a big drink of his coffee before he got started.

"We can show you where it came from once we finish devouring whatever smells so amazing. As for what it does, we're still trying to figure that out. My cousin has my grandmother's notebooks from the assisted living, so we're hoping what she wrote will help."

He paused to open the lid, revealing the satiny smooth wood inside. And nothing else.

By the time he finished talking, Quinn had refilled everyone's cups, and Jeri and Bev wore nearly identical expressions of wonder.

"So you think this has been…showing the possibilities for your family for several generations?" Jeri said. "And now it belongs to you?"

Doug lifted both shoulders and turned his head to the side.

"That's what I *think*, but we only found it yesterday. Besides what my grandmother wrote, I was thinking we might try to figure out more. Trace it back as best we can. Maybe take a trip to England and see what we can find."

Even though she'd been lucky enough to go overseas several times, Quinn's heart leapt at the chance to make that journey with Doug. They'd talked about it many times, but only as daydreams.

The reality of the change in her life hit her in a new wave of excitement and pleasure.

"I'm sorry you never got to hear all of it from your grandmother," Bev said. "Sounds like she was sorry too."

A jolt of reality in an unreal situation yanked Quinn in the opposite emotional direction. Her passage into menopause had been as routine as such things get, and over a year ago.

A biological reality she'd never much been bothered by until now.

"I truly hate to be the one to mention this," she said, rubbing Doug's arm, "but this time capsule seems to pass along within your family. That's not something we could do much about. Not easily, anyway. Not with me."

He shook his head and caught her hand, holding it tight in both of his. She couldn't look away from his lovely green eyes.

"I'm not about to spend time worrying about that. Not now, and not ever. If this magic box is meant to be passed along, I suspect it's perfectly capable of telling us so. If we're being painfully honest, I didn't exactly do my familial duty over the years. By the time I turned thirty, I had made damn sure not to. Okay?"

Before Quinn could answer, Jeri reached toward the box and stopped. Her eyes were wide, and a blush highlighted her pale cheeks.

"I'm sorry, that was terribly presumptuous of me," she said. "May I?"

Quinn laughed before she could stop herself, relieved at the break from her personal tension.

"I'll happily take the bonus points in my evaluation," Doug said, smiling and pushing the box over. "Be my guest."

"You should see her in the kitchen," Bev said, leaning her shoulder against Jeri's. "Always trying to sneak around when I'm working on a new recipe."

Jeri stuck out her tongue as she gently raised the box's lid.

"And sometimes my suggestions make all the difference. Hey, it's not empty now."

All of them leaned forward when Jeri took out a handful of thick, cream-colored envelopes, with embossed writing glittering.

"Did you…" Bev said, staring at Doug.

"You were here the whole time," he said, raising Quinn's hand and his other one. "Neither of us touched it."

Jeri handed two envelopes to Bev, and one each to Quinn and Doug.

"If you just found this yesterday," Jeri said, "there's no way you got all this done."

"They're addressed to us," Bev said, her voice light and wondering. "One from Atlanta and one from your house, Quinn."

Quinn's heartbeat sped up when she looked at the one in her hand.

"Mine is addressed to here, to this house. From Quinn Hedges and Doug Linton, who live in my house."

Doug's eyes were wide when he met her gaze.

"I've got one from my place in Atlanta to here, from both of us."

Quinn winked at him, then smiled at Jeri and Bev.

"There's only one way to solve this little mystery."

All four of them opened the envelopes at once. And a few seconds later, they all held up party invitations decorated with balloons, streamers, and various images of the number five.

"You're inviting us to a birthday party," Bev said, "on the same day, at the same time, in St. Louis and Atlanta."

Jeri's brow wrinkled. "I'm sorry to be so clueless, but should I know who Ian is?"

Doug rubbed the back of his neck, shaking his head slowly.

"I don't see how you would know, since he's less

than a week old. Ian is my cousin Jenny's first grandchild. I haven't even met him yet."

Quinn took a bit longer to find her voice through the waves of wonder moving through her, with ghostly tingles of awe and a tiny bit of fear mixed in.

"Ian is also the reason Doug showed up for the walkthrough the other day instead of his cousin. Otherwise I probably would have chatted with her for a few hours, given her my appraisal, and helped sell the house. And that would have been the end of it. Maybe with this time capsule or magic box or whatever it is hidden away in the sub-basement forever."

Doug stared into her eyes with a crooked smile.

"Did you notice the date?"

Quinn, Bev, and Jeri looked back down and let out a collective sigh.

"Just short of five years from now," Bev said, shaking her head. "Around the time his Grandmama Jenny would be happy to give Mom and Dad a break if he's like most kids that age. I thought you said your time capsule doesn't tell the future?"

Doug laughed and sat back.

"I should have said none of the things *we* found in there did that. For all I know, my grandmother saw the future every day. Maybe she saw things that won't happen for years."

"Maybe she saw *possible* futures," Quinn said, turning her envelope over in her hands. "We can't possibly host this party on the same day in two different states, just like those anniversaries we saw couldn't have all happened."

"Sounds to me like you might have solved one of your mysteries," Jeri said. "If Ian is showing up already, maybe he's the one the time capsule will focus on next."

All of them jumped when Bev's phone buzzed on the counter beside the stove. She glared at Doug and Quinn in turn.

"Just let me say this before you stampede over here to get this brunch in your bellies. If you do decide to have little Ian's party in St. Louis when the time comes for number five or any time before that, Auntie Bev better be at the top of the list for handling the catering."

All four of them got to their feet, with signs that "stampede" was the right word. Quinn slipped her arm around Doug's waist and leaned into his arm around her shoulder.

"If we're here," she said, "there won't be any list, Auntie Bev. We'd never consider asking anyone else. Right?"

Doug gave her a quick kiss and leaned his forehead against hers.

"Right, even if the food is only half as good as it smells. Listen, I'm not in the business of guessing the future either, but I gotta ask. I don't suppose you know anyone who might be willing to help an engineer explore the local job market? Just in case."

Quinn shifted until they stood cheek to cheek and she could whisper into his ear.

"I happen to know a local realtor who would love to help."

ABOUT KARI

Kari and her husband Jason A. Adams met in a computer lab in college in 1990 and proceeded to live out several enduring romance tropes, including rebound romance, friends into lovers, young love, and even second chance romance when they divorced and remarried, all before the end of the 90s. So it was perhaps inevitable that they'd both end up writing romance.

Kari also writes fantasy, science fiction, and contemporary fiction, and she's happiest when she surprises herself. She lives at the end of a long dirt road in the middle of the woods with Jason, various house critters, and wildlife they're better off not knowing more about.

The Confidential Adventure Club

For Kari's exclusive free After The End stories and deleted scenes, discounts, early pre-sale releases, adorable pet photos, and a whole lot more not available anywhere else, swing by

www.ConfidentialAdventureClub.com.

Hope to see you there!

www.KariKilgore.com
www.SpiralPublishing.net

ALSO BY KARI KILGORE

I hope you enjoyed reading *The Box of Possibilities* as much as I enjoyed writing it. You'll find more romance short stories, novellas, and novels to come at www.KariKilgore.com/Romance.

Be the first to know about release dates and check out more of my fiction, including almost every genre with plenty of romantic elements, at www.KariKilgore.com.

The Confidential Adventure Club

Want more fiction from Kari, including stories, discounts, and box sets not available anywhere else? Want to hear about locations, research, and other cool things that inspired this story and beyond? Want all that and adorable pet photos, too?

Join The Confidential Adventure Club and get a thank you gift of a free short story and a whole lot more. www.ConfidentialAdventureClub.com.

Hope to see you there!

The Storms of Future Past Series:

Dreaming the Storm

Joining the Storm

Into the Storm

Fighting the Storm

Sensing the Storm: A Storms of Future Past Prequel

Storms of the Heart: A Storms of Future Past Romance

Storms of Future Past Books One through Four Collection

The Odd Society:

Independent by Means of Magic

Protected by Means of Magic

The Voices through Time Series:

Songs in the Mountain

Secrets in the Land

Walking the Ghosts: A Voices through Time Novella

Dispatches from the Galaxy Stories:

Restricted Species

The Becalmed

The Garbage Belt

Plurapod Pathogen

The Changes Cascade

Novels:

Until Death

The Dream Thief

Hand Me Downs

Protecting Her Own

Novellas:

Legacy of the Land

In the Pines

DNA Never Lies

Collections:

Fantastic Women: A Dark Fantasy Novella Trio

Fantastic Shorts: Volume 1

Near Future Forward (with Jason A. Adams)

Fantastic Shorts: Volume 2

Partners in Romance (with Jason A. Adams)

Dispatches from the Galaxy: A Space Opera Novella Trio

Fantastic Shorts: Volume 3

Escape into Romance: A Collection of Sweet Beginnings

9 781948 890731